THE FARMHOUSE ON CEMETERY HILL ROAD

CYNTHIA HERBERT BRUSCHI ADAMS

ISBN: 978-1-64184-460-4 (Paperback)
ISBN: 978-1-64184-461-1 (eBook)

DEDICATION

To Priscilla D. Douglas a friend who encouraged and praised my work before I even began and to my editor-in-chief and dear husband Roger A. Adams for his continual support and love.

ACKNOWLEDGEMENTS

No one could have had finer readers than I. Beginning with Dr. Willie Hagan, a retired university president and current screenplay writer who read and analyzed the manuscript giving me the feedback necessary for a story to succeed or fail: a retired university professor, Dr. Susan Spiggle who is still reviewing graduate research papers; a retired English teacher and school principal, Ann Aulerich, who sees everything but delivers the news with kindness; a current author, Sharon Cormier, who is very Zen and extremely willing to edit and share all her ideas for success; to those like Dr. Edith Posselt, retired psychologist, who let me know it was a hard book to put down and very scary; and last but not least my son Andrew H. Adams, who himself is clever with the pen and business and who lived in two antique houses with his dad and me as he grew up; he too finds this compelling and frightening. I thank you more than you will ever imagine. Working on this during the Pandemic but knowing you folks were there was an enriching experience like no other.

CONTENTS

1

DISCOVERIES

I'd been calling the cat for three days with no response. I put a plate of food out hoping the scent would draw her back. But on that fourth morning although the food was gone it hadn't been the cat that ate it: her lifeless, matted body was lying beside the empty dish. I started berating myself for having let her go outside. We'd lived in this rundown antique home for little over a week and I knew cats are so territorial they take a long time to adjust to a new place. Still she had rushed to any door that we had opened seeming to demand a chance for fresh air. She was so anxious to go out that I mistakenly assumed she could handle the experience. We had many wooded acres behind us. Surely she wanted to chase mice or voles and climb a tree or explore the barn. But the front of the house was near a road and the woods were rife with predators; she had succumbed to something. Poor Diamond kitty I thought. She had been a tuxedo cat, all black and white; with a diamond shaped patch next to her nose thus earning her the glamorous title. She had been a lovely pet that I should not have let out so soon.

Now the atmosphere seemed a bit tainted. For the first time I felt something was wrong. This foreboding was tied to the cat in part because I had no idea what or possibly who had brought her back to the house. But were there really other disturbing signs giving me this feeling? I needed to get outside and begin the tasks I'd intended doing and not dwell on this loss. Matt could help me bury her later. I just needed to be busy and that would cheer me up

Part of living in this farmhouse on Cemetery Hill Rd. included exploring the grounds as well as the structure. Back in the eighteenth century people had no shared dumps or trash collectors. Leftover food was fed to the pigs which helped to fatten them. Nothing was wasted and the pigs would, in a sense, recycle the food into ham and bacon which would then feed the family again or lead to money when the meat was sold at local markets. If the pig wouldn't eat something it was tossed in a mulch pile where it could decay and later be used as fertilizer on the gardens. This mulching method would return nutrients to the soil thus stimulating growth of the coming year's crops. After generations had used the same area for mulch collection it wasn't unusual to find small "treasures" packed in among the rotted food such as spoons or ladles that had made an escape out with the offal. And if the cook was missing a ring it was likely in a sow's belly or within this fetid pile.

Similarly glassware which had outlived its usefulness would be buried in the backyard typically under stone walls or around shrub thickets so the glass itself would not cut anyone but remain out of the way. This led to the common practice of bottle digging by twentieth century folks wanting to find "antiques". It was very common in New England to dig around an old stone wall and discover small glass flasks which had contained various elixirs, potions, or alcohol all purportedly used for health benefits. Some of the containers were rather pretty,

2

some even colored amber, brown or green, and a few would be found intact. The possibility of finding these treasures to help embellish our new home led me to use a trowel around the stone walls.

Matt and I were still practically newlyweds and I had a strong nesting instinct for this, the first home we had purchased. These items would provide an instant sense of history and permanence. I wanted a solid marriage that would last forever like this well-built old farmhouse.

First I found part of a pretty teacup and half of its saucer. Then I discovered the rest of both the cup and saucer so that with a little washing and gluing I might have something unique and complete to display. Next I found an old horseshoe and quickly hung it on the smokehouse door with the ends up and the curve below so that the luck would not run out. I don't know if I believed this old superstition but why take a chance. Next there were several unrecognizable shards of glass, perhaps old inkwells, which were common but nearly always shattered. Anything that was whole I planned on placing in a window so that light passing through it would lend a timeless glow to the antique house. It seemed to me that I was almost being called into the yard to find and return these artifacts to the home: these items had been used there and belonged inside. Their purpose would now be to decorate the home of origin: there was symmetry to their being returned even several generations later. And the artifacts crying out to me gave me a sense of transcending time. Then I started finding bones.

Naturally I reasoned, this being an old farmstead, of course these were animal remains. There were large femur type bones, bone fragments, curved bones but no skulls. The lack of skulls was disappointing as I imagined cleaning them and displaying them in rather an Arizonian/desert fashion and also as the cranium and nostril openings would help to identify just what creature I was unearthing.

Also there was the "why". Why were these bones so close to the house? Had there been a barn right here or was this the part of the farmland used for slaughter or disposal of cattle as they were prepared for cooking and then consumed? When I reinterred these seemingly ordinary bone bits I quickly crossed myself saying a little prayer for the dead. My mother being 100 percent Italian, and my having been raised as a Catholic in Roma as Elena Maria, never mind the Anglo last name, left me stuck with a number of deeply held beliefs and practices. I remain basically unconsciously stuck with these rituals and only notice them when my husband points them out.

I continued to dig. It became almost addictive; would I find anything that day, what message would the object or pieces convey? When I got to the point where nails, metal keg hoops and broken axes were all that I was finding I'd move up the stone wall to ground I had yet to break. Then, on my third day of exploring, and three days after Diamond's body came home, three things happened.

The first was a fine rash that grew from my wrists up my arms. I had been wearing gardening gloves to help avoid cuts during this endeavor but my arms were mostly bare as it was late spring and the work soon made me hot. Apparently some of the vines I had cavalierly yanked out of my way were actually the dreaded poison ivy plant. I had been warned to avoid this weed with the three small shiny leaves but it was obviously too early in the growth season to see these markers of trouble. So I foolishly ripped vines out with no heed as to where their juices might land on me. Any part of my body that wasn't protected was infected and that involved one side of my neck and face. The more I scratched the rash the more it demanded to be scratched and rapidly spread beyond the exposed areas. I started contemplating quitting for a while. It was a maddening sensation and by now I couldn't help but rub dirt into it.

The second thing would have stopped me completely if it were not for the third. Sitting on top of the next portion of stone wall was a snake warming itself in the afternoon sun. Realistically it was no more than five feet long but my emotional eye thought I was seeing a nine foot monster. It was black and shiny but did not seem to rattle. I've never had a huge fear of snakes, so long as I know them to not be poisonous, but it was the surreptitiousness of this serpent – it just laid there as though I wouldn't see it or wouldn't mind sharing my afternoon with it; I saw it as a demon. It didn't seem to have the decency to show fear of the human species and get out of the way. I did not consider just working quietly beside it, digging cupfuls of soil and shaking them through a sieve, as a sensible act on my part. If the poison ivy plant had snuck up on me as it had, then why indeed would I trust a snake?

As I was about to bolt for the door, dreaming of iced tea and Calamine Lotion, something long, white and flat appeared under the weeds and roots just beyond my current spot. It was much larger than any bottles I had found and even larger than a dinner plate. Once determining that I was well away from the reptile on the stones I settled down near the object. It was only shallowly covered with a few weeds, moss and dirt. Within moments I had dusted off its face using my gloved hands alone to be certain not to chip or damage this item. It was enormous; at least as long as the snake simply based on what was uncovered, and two feet wide. It was flat and engraved and also decorated with a few pictures including a book and a candle. The words formed a poem and contained two dates 1811 – 1823: I had unearthed a gravestone!

The name on the stone appeared to be "Wilbur" then perhaps a surname which was illegible, then "Beloved Son" and those dates. I could make out most of the words in the poem.

Shed not for him a single tear
Spare not for him your regret
'Tis but the body that lies here
The soul that graced it
Wanders yet!

Good Heavens! A gravestone declaring a wandering soul and was this the site of the actual grave or were body and soul in different locations; or did the soul remain with the corpse? Mama Mia, another find like this and I'll have to go hunt for my rosary! I desperately wanted to know where the body was right way. The realtor had mentioned nothing about our own graveyard although the street is named Cemetery Hill Road. I had assumed that somewhere on the street, perhaps behind a barn or in an old cornfield, there was a small abandoned family plot, nothing of consequence and certainly not on our property!

Pushing the gloves off my hands and then wiping them as best I could on my dungarees, I dug out my cell phone and prepared to take a picture of the stone. I was sending this unbelievable photo to Matt at work. Maybe he could get home sooner if he knew his wife was about to dig up a grave. In any case I was very relieved to see that the picture turned out as I had seen it with the naked eye, no fading image and no strange aura appearing around the stone; nothing from a vampire novel. After sending it off to Matt I decided it really was time to go into the house.

The house itself is a large Colonial style home, originally a farmhouse, built around a central chimney and with two ells attached at the back. It must have originally been painted red for that color was still obvious through chips and faded images which clung to the clapboards. It sits high on the land and is three stories tall so that at almost any point on the property you could orient yourself by looking up and around until you found the rooftop on the horizon. On this afternoon I entered through a back shed that led down a hallway to the kitchen. Each time I entered our new home even from a short stay in the yard, I was reminded just how much work lay ahead. Friends had teased us about buying "a money pit". They all seemed to prefer modern homes with level floors, windows that convert from storm to screen and air conditioning along with central vacuuming. Those luxuries all sounded good to us but Matt and I were intrigued by history and the notion of restoring a place to its nearly original condition. There was beauty and charm to heating much of a home with fireplaces and developing accurate images of how the homes of those days would look right on down from paint to rugs and upholstered furniture in between. It took research to garner these facts but we knew folks who enjoyed blacksmithing, chimney building, basket weaving and all aspects of restoration.

I'm sure the psychology of the "old house aficionado" is fairly obvious. These houses give off not only a sense of permanence but of deep roots. Look how long they have existed; this house shouts "family" from its rafters with the cozy fireplaces and the charming bedrooms, and that is what we wanted. Our house is more than a domicile, it is a homestead! You are home when you are here and we both wanted a place our future children would return to because it was warm and loving.

In terms of restoration we were also fortunate enough to live in the part of New England that not only had many older homes from which to model our work, but that promoted restoration and offered excellent reproduction items such as chandeliers and other light fixtures; furniture and general household items. Lately we had become excited by the hardware on doors; finding original latches added to the appeal of a door and the door to its room. Sturbridge Village, Old Deerfield and even Salem, Massachusetts were an easy commute. One of these experts had discussed how we would match today's paints against the original paint on the front banister. His advice was that we could not match the paint but rather would need to make it just as it had been made over 200 plus years ago. White paint was sold commercially but color variations had to be created by what existed on the farm. Berries were frequently used as dye however our desired shade of red was a mixture of milk and ox blood. The name "ox blood" even continues on some color charts today. A little disconcerting to think animal blood was smeared onto our walls. It was difficult to decide just how to tackle this color issue.

Perhaps my work in the yard was a way to avoid the effort, decisions and expense which were hanging over us as we began to make this old house solid and livable. I would make an attack plan for this work once I figured out if somebody with "Wilbur" in his name was interred in the backyard. In any case I was too dirty to enter through the ell to the dining room and wanted to reach the deep kitchen soapstone sink as quickly as possible. Once there I gently deposited the day's treasures in the sink and allowed water to collect in the bottom to soak them. You never want to drop glassware into a soapstone sink as it is very solid and unforgiving. Probably the reason these useful sinks are not currently in fashion is due to the damage that can quickly ruin your family heirloom china.

Now, I asked myself, how do I proceed? Checking my phone I saw there was no response from Matt so I was on my own. If I had "Wilbur's" full name I could look at Town Records but in this case I didn't know if I had a first, last, or middle name. This farmstead was close to 250 years old. I presumed that rules for burial probably didn't exist back then. If a family wanted to keep a deceased child "at home" and had ample land then there was likely nothing to prevent them from a home burial. Although there were certainly churches in the community and old graveyards it did not necessarily follow that everyone clove to those locations. I knew that during Colonial times the family made pomander balls if a loved one passed away during winter. These balls were made from oranges stuffed with cloves and dusted with cinnamon and preservatives. The orange juice soaked into the cloves and cinnamon creating a strong pleasant odor to help mask the decaying of the corpse.

Using pomander balls was never a first choice but could be a necessity when the long winter months kept the ground frozen solid in old New England. It was always hoped that "Auntie's body" could also be stored away from the family if space permitted. Attic space or a cold shed had many advantages for such storage while the cellar presented too many opportunities for vermin and mold. The more desperate and crowded families would place the body in a corner or a cupboard necessitating the frequent production of more scented balls and a general disgust with the atmosphere.

But my chief concern right now must be how to proceed in learning of Wilbur and his remains. There was an older lady near the top of the hill who had been born in that house and whose parents had spent most of their lives on the Hill. She seemed to know everything. I proceeded to give Priscilla a call.

Priscilla was probably 5'5" tall and very soft looking. That is her flesh held no tone but rather her muscles hung like loose cords running down her arms. Her hair was curled but not really styled and her dresses might have been new around the beginning of WWII, well before I was conceived. Her teeth rattled in her mouth and the lenses on her spectacles appeared to be magnifying glasses. As unkind as this physical description might sound I had great respect for her.

She was a serious, bright and hardworking person and never wasted money on superficial things although she was rumored to be quite well-to-do and knew everyone through the many organizations in which she participated. She also collected antique glassware and ran a secondhand/antique shop out of her old dairy barn so she was a wonderful source of information and treasures.

There were two levels to her shop. The larger downstairs area had been converted from old cattle stalls which now served as borders around different types of items. For example, two collapsed stalls housed dressers and corner cupboards; another was boxes of silver, pewter and mostly silver plated items; and a third was glassware, the better pieces displayed in a case. But the upstairs was off limits to physical contact. Surrounding the upstairs rail you could see a display of the very best antiques and know that they were not for sale!

Here there were beautifully wood crafted cribs, rocking horses, cradles and fine furniture. These items had been left by Priscilla's family or she had spotted them as superior at auctions and bought them simply to own. No one interested in old homes and antiques could look up without coveting these treasures. She would follow your eyes and say "oh my Grandfather carved that but it is not for sale" and no amount of begging, bargaining or cajoling would dissuade her from hanging onto the item in question. Whatever she was willing to sell from her downstairs collection was never as good as what taunted you from the upstairs.

While we spoke she explained that there was indeed a cemetery on our street. She guessed Wilbur might actually be buried there reasoning that as he died when a child his family might have erected "my" stone for him in the cemetery to begin with and then had a family stone, which included him, once they were all in the graveyard. So his original stone was brought back to the house when it was replaced. I must have indicated surprise at this because she quickly added "we all end up in the grave soon enough." At the end of this call I hurriedly got myself together and, leaving a note for Matt while grabbing the directions I had jotted down, set out to see this cemetery.

2

THE CEMETERY

Priscilla indicated the cemetery was only slightly off the street as the hill bends east, and just behind a barn. She assured me it was visible from the roadway. She said it was the old town cemetery and therefore any citizen had the right to walk onto its grounds. Although I fancied myself fairly athletic I rarely walked as far as these four miles and never willingly did eight. For some reason I always found it more entertaining to walk on cobblestones; so I drove up to spare myself the four mile roundtrip hike, and because I was anxious to get there. Now knowing where to look I found it quickly and was amazed I had not spotted it on other sojourns although I rarely had to follow the road on this easterly route

There were probably 50 head stones in various stages of decay. None of them stood perfectly upright and several were actually lying on the ground. All were darkened, thin and crumbling or missing their facades or the chiseled words had been worn away by acid rain. Still it was possible to see some names and dates. There was one large stone clearly marking the area of a family plot. I thought this must be where Wilbur and his kin lay only to be disappointed that no member of the family bore even the slightest hint of using the name Wilbur at least on the stones where the engraving was intact. It was, however, a very poignant spot as one family had lost five children each one dying before the age of two. I could not imagine how the parents remained sane and tried again to have children only to have more loss. Of course there was no genetic testing back then or birth control; a sad realization.

As intriguing as this information was it brought me no closer to knowing where Wilbur might currently reside. I decided to take a few photographs and head back home. On my way to the car "the cousin" of my black snake slithered out from under a loose stone. I came very close to dropping my cell phone and running; instead I moved slowly with an eye on the serpent as it slithered back under its stones in reaction to my motion. Once I was safely ensconced again in my car I certainly said another little prayer.

It was time to fix dinner. Matt should be home from the University by 6 pm unless his students held him up with questions or problems. He was a dedicated teacher and this being his tenure year he was attempting to excel in all areas: research, teaching and service. It was probably not the best time for us to have bought our first home and to be trying to have a baby but too many clocks were ticking us toward the "normal life" of thirty-somethings. I loved Matt passionately so when he was due at home I always grew excited.

I had met Matt five years ago when I was a college freshman. He was the teaching assistant for the Introductory to Psychology course I was taking. Small groups of us had to do laboratory work with him. Right away I thought he was cute and even possibly "the one" as I told my mother while home in Italy over Christmas break, but he was a graduate student and I was a freshman so chances seemed slim. During the second semester he was again my group's TA. This attraction spurred an intense interest in psychology. I wanted to be the one who had the right answers and who was also helpful to my fellow students. I also stopped rolling out of bed just fifteen minutes before class time and throwing a trench coat over my pajamas. I needed plenty of time to be well groomed with sparkling teeth if I was going to attract this guy.

I had always been told I was "bella" because Italian mamas and zias are open, affectionate and demonstrative. They were always pinching my cheeks, hugging and kissing me. It certainly enhanced a sense of positive self-esteem but once I was on new turf with a mature American graduate student I felt a little shy.

Matt seemed to find me amusing and we developed some rapport. I was glad he was tall because I am considered tall by Italian standards. I would get to class early and have coffee with him while he set up for teaching but he didn't call or ask me out. I was careful not to overdo my part by making up course questions or problems. I did not want to be labeled as a stalker or seen as unfit for future positions in psychology so I held back. Still I would wear my shortest skirts or shorts to class and noted when his eyes seemed to be on my legs, even briefly. Then the semester came to an end and I had not made great strides on my quest to become important to him. Once back home for the summer with my father, in Rhode Island, my dad asked me how it had gone and I simply replied that my social life had been limited to pizza with friends on Friday nights.

After about a week a card came in the mail. It was from Matt but it was a preprinted message with only his signature. It read on the cover: "I miss you like crazy" and inside it concluded: "You know how I like crazy!" Was this psychologist humor? It seemed I could take it as a cautious sign of interest but what to do? Matt solved that by calling the next day and asking if he could visit. He said while I was a student he didn't want to set up a conflict of interest but he was interested in taking me out.

Soon he confided that my legs had driven him crazy and he found everything about me cute. I questioned "cute?" and his response was "Well, okay, sexy, gorgeous and captivating." I said "gracie" and also returned several compliments regarding his good looks and intelligence but the most significant thing that happened was his passionate kisses, really passionate.

We were engaged by Christmas and married at the end of my sophomore year. Then we took an apartment and went about the tasks of my finishing a bachelor's degree and Matt completing his dissertation. Both of these were taking place in Rhode Island but Matt's completed doctorate allowed him to begin a faculty position over the border at the University of Connecticut while we remained in the apartment and tried to squirrel away money for the down-payment on a house.

Now I was anxious to have a meal ready so our focus tonight could be on my big discovery of a possible body in the yard. I wanted Matt as excited about this house and our future here as was I. I hoped hamburger casserole would do as it contained meat, vegetable and potato. If we had enough lettuce I'd add a salad to keep him well fed before making the great announcement. He might need energy to take this all in.

As things were we had a barely functional kitchen. The previous owner hadn't cooked here in years. The refrigerator worked but we'd had to scrape it out and sanitize it before actually placing food inside. There was one counter top available for preparations; all other surfaces held boxes of stores from our old apartment. This kitchen had been gutted of anything resembling a cupboard. We had set boards on bricks to hold most canned goods and cookware.

Still the room contained the most beautiful large original fireplace; one which you could practically walk into. We had just found that boarded up behind a wall.

Our carpenter friend, Fred, had come with us to see the house immediately after we took ownership. We had met him in RI as he did the repairs and upgrades for our then landlord. He seemed pretty much a loner but was always interested in staying for dinner or having lunch with us if we were around while he was working. He was a bit gaunt but mostly muscular; acting so happy and free it was impossible to guess his age.

Over time we learned that he had been married later in life to a woman who stayed around as long as he had money. He had been living frugally for years until she was in the picture and when she demanded a nice home he gave it to her. At one point she brought her two adult children to live with them and those "kids" helped make the money disappear. Friends could see he was being taken for a ride but his innocent outlook made him deny that she would do him any wrong. After a few years he had to confess that there wasn't much cash left and she and her brood were gone within a week.

He never seemed bitter just very independent. A sweet man really who referred to one of his hammers as "his pet". He wanted his freedom to come and go as he pleased so the less we tried to pin him down about when a project might be completed, the more he did for us. He was so independent that he found cheap accommodations near us and just moved to our area when we bought this old place. He took other jobs but he knew this house would mean steady employment without much hassle. There were also few jobs he could not do although it was understood that he might not be licensed in all. In that respect he functioned more like an "Uncle" helping us out. It seemed that whatever family he was working for at the time became his surrogate family; and when he had another big job the next folks would then serve as family. But unlike his ex-wife, he never forgot the folks he had worked with.

So that day we had begun with the location of the central chimney. We reasoned there must have been a kitchen fireplace within a certain parameter of that chimney. But Fred was cautious not wanting us to be disappointed. He explained he had known many houses of this vintage to have had the fireplaces removed once families bought gas stoves. And the fact that there was no hearth stone protruding into the room was an indication that no fireplace still existed.

I had been too enchanted by the notion of the kitchen fireplace to give up on the idea so, rather than to bash in a kitchen wall only to be required to replace it, Fred got a flashlight and went into the cellar. Matt and I asked if we should join him but he said "go stand where you think the fireplace will be and just yell to me when you see the light". We waited and then shouted "yes" in unison. We heard an "okay" and then he was back in the kitchen. "Okay what" we asked? Fred's response: "There is a large stone slab right where a hearth should be. I think someone dropped it down and covered it with them oak boards you are standin' on."

"Then you think the fireplace is still here?" I had asked. "Well" he said, "I think it is worth lookin'." Matt moved things away from the wall and Fred and I got a mallet and a crowbar. Within twenty minutes we had found a fabulous fireplace complete with a cooking arm and next to it a beehive oven! We felt like we had reached the Titanic!

"While you're in a good mood" Fred injected, "I'd say you got a prize crop of spiders in that cellar of yours." I had found the cellar a bit creepy and webby and had not concentrated on it but was suddenly taking his point that there might be both cleaning and exterminating to do. We'd have to get this on the list along with insulating the house, replacing drafty windows and actually having a working kitchen. Not a top priority but important.

So in the face of this beautiful granite and brick fireplace which Fred had helped us discover I was now preparing the night's dinner on top of boxes and trunks. What I really wanted to do was get Matt's opinion on who Wilbur might be and where we should be hunting for his remains, but I would have to wait.

Just after six Matt arrived home and was pleased to find I had dusted off a space and set up what could pass for a dining area. He spoke of his day and how many papers he would need to grade that evening. Finally I told him of my explorations, the uncovering of "Wilbur's" stone and the graveyard I had visited based on Priscilla's directions. He didn't disappoint me when he stood up and said, "Let's go see that monument!"

We went out behind the house and along the stone wall now strewn with bits of glass and metal from my diggings; then we were on the gravestone. Matt whistled sounding impressed. He bent down and tried to dig around its edges but found the stone both too thick and too imbedded in the earth. He guessed we wouldn't be standing it upright without equipment and help. I explained that it did not appear that Wilbur's family was buried up the hill. Maybe he is right here Matt conjectured then sighed and said we'd better call Larry, our attorney, to see if he'd forgotten to mention something interesting showing up during the title search. I stammered "Will we need to bury him properly on consecrated ground?" Matt replied that I was way over reacting. "Wherever he lies," said Matt "He should be allowed to rest in peace."

By noon the next day we were assured the title search had nothing to add to this mystery but Larry's office was aware of another graveyard on the street. Two graveyards, I thought, no wonder this is called

Cemetery Hill Road! And so with Matt at his office I again headed out to find and hunt through the new graveyard.

This burial place was very well hidden. It was downhill from us and on the opposite side of the street along what appeared to be a backyard path between two properties. Once I walked behind the tree line there was a little clearing with only eight headstones showing. Fieldstones were formed in a rectangle around those headstones and the entry point was simply a gap between them. Right away I drew up short seeing a marker that partially blocked this tiny path. The marker bore the only legible wording that was visible from this angle and read "All Souls Lost Here Due to the Smallpox Epidemic of 1867. These bodies remain quarantined and all wise men pay heed or unleash grief upon the earth and a curse upon your kin."

I jumped back ten feet! While I wanted to read the names I wasn't sure if 150 years was long enough to have removed the poison of the epidemic. I checked with my cell phone for contamination information on the web and then moved forward to look more closely. There was nothing fancy about these grave markers. All must have been hastily engraved to fulfill a need during an emergency. Once again I did not find Wilbur's name. He had died well ahead of his family, surely not as part of an epidemic. Wherever he or his relatives might be it was not in this smallpox cemetery. A shiver went down my spine; I hoped I would not be cursed for intruding on this very private feeling gravesite.

I returned home to reconsider the possibilities and to ponder the many other duties I seemed to be avoiding while pursuing Wilbur's location. I called Priscilla again to see if she had thought of anything since our last conversation. She offered that there had been some kind of family issue with the people who had lived in the house nearest to the one we now owned. When they had moved away there had been a lingering problem of some sort. What could this have to do with my missing corpse from 1823, I asked her. She said there was some connection but could say no more. She then advised me to contact my realtor. This was rather baffling but I'd come this far, why not see what thoughts she was hiding from me, yet sending clues.

Adam, our realtor, was a hardworking and cautious man probably about my age. He liked to do everything by the book and follow rules so that none could find him unethical. He had been a kind and supportive partner to Matt and me as we spent considerable time finding this "ideal home". Actually we had been looking for this dream house for nearly three years. It was taking extra time because the dream wasn't well funded, that is, we wanted a lot of house for not very much money. When we looked at an affordable home which appeared to have the correct characteristics there was always some surprise detractor. Like the spacious house which was built around a ballroom with 20 foot high ceilings and, it was an all-electric home; no reasonably priced renovations could make this either a cozy place or an economical one.

Other disappointments occurred regarding the land we wished to have with the home. A house might be intriguing but the next door neighbor could reach out her window and turn on our light fixtures or plug her vacuum into our wall socket. No privacy and certainly no space for gardening or genteel landscaping. We might have a nice home but would feel rather like mortar squished in between bricks. The dream definitely included acres of land surrounding the home. We figured we were being frugal by not seeking an ocean view but naturally we would have needed to stay in RI for there to have been any probability of success with that and certainly not in our income range.

Then there were the advertisements which spoke of three or more bedroom houses on 12 spacious acres of land in the country with an easy commute to neighboring towns. One such abode honestly had the space but the home sat on top of a steep hill. We would become the proud owners of the hill but there wasn't enough flat land that came with the property to even set up a lawn chair for fear of rolling down said hill and into the brambles or the street.

And of course we must not forget "location, location, location". That phrase became a damning thought when the perfect, spacious, multi-acred home was planted on a highway or at the intersection of two or more busy roadways. We had never dreamed of fast-food hamburger chains as neighbors. Nor had we imagined the home nearest to us having a kennel full of small yippy dogs which seemed to bark incessantly and especially if any vehicle pulled onto the property we were considering.

Adam did not seem perturbed by our reluctance to make a decision. He was patient throughout this time. He seemed to appreciate the spot we were in financially and did not have a need to rush us. This support made it possible for us to continue the hunt and to bond with Adam as both a friend and realtor. The pursuit was exciting yet the criteria we had set, combined with the small bank account, were daunting. But after each disappointment Adam never said "If you can't come up with more money you'd better learn to settle", or any such suggestion as other realtors had made to our friends. Rather, he'd say not to worry, there were plenty of houses out there and sooner or later everything comes on the market. He assured us he would continue the hunt until we were satisfied.

Progress in home selection was moving slowly until a friend mentioned that a house in her neighborhood was going on the market as the owner, an elderly lady in nursing care, had just passed away. She also said the house was built in the 1700s and had charm. It was a post and beam colonial with multiple fireplaces, out buildings, and an option to buy much of the farmland that had always been part of it. She didn't know what the asking price would be but several relatives were anxious to get something out of the sale so perhaps it would be reasonable, plus the departed owner had not been able to keep up the repairs for some time. Might this equal a bargain she speculated?

I knew the general location so later that day Matt and I took a ride by the house. He was horrified by the chipping paint and mossy roof but I fell instantly in love. The age of the house only made it more endearing to me, lent mystery and challenge. I wanted to be significant to this property's history, uncover its secrets and its flaws and breathe new life into this curious relic. I knew we had to get inside and thus called Adam from my cell phone to get us in as soon as possible.

Now I called Adam with a much different request. What did he know about the house, the people and the history of the home next door?

3

BUMP IN THE NIGHT

Adam's first comment was a light one. "Gee I thought you were inviting us to dinner or had decided the place was too much work and wanted a refund." Of course he knew we were hardly operational so there would be a long delay before we entertained and we were so nuts about this house that even offers of large amounts of money could not tear us from this quest. So when I told him we wanted to hear about the old Macintosh family who had lived next door he only said "Ok, I'll be right over." Was there something he didn't want to say on the phone or send in an email I wondered?

Ten minutes later Adam was at the door. By way of an explanation he only laughed, "Slow day for real estate. Now what can I do for you, Elena Maria?" I started at the beginning about uncovering a tombstone while digging for relics in the earth around our stone wall. I explained that led me to question Priscilla Austin from the top of the hill, and then to explore two cemeteries on our street. He took all this in stride until I added, but I could find no person named "Wilbur" and I want to know where the body is.

"This is a little out of my field", he said amicably; "I haven't been involved in body snatching since my college days." "Very funny", I rejoined. "Adam, no one thinks you took the body but rumor has it you may know something about it perhaps related to the Macintoshes."

He began by saying that the Macintoshes were a very nice family who had lived on Cemetery Hill Road since well before he was born. They had built the house next door so it really was a contemporary dwelling, beautiful kitchen, great floor plan. Before he could go further I jumped in and reminded him that we didn't want to buy their home, just to learn something about what could possibly connect them to "our" Wilbur.

"Well", he went on, "after Professor Macintosh retired, she and her husband decided to move to Kentucky where she had family. They refreshed the paint in their home, refurbished the deck and cleaned out the garage. It wasn't long before several potential buyers were interested in the place…it was just a few years ago, maybe you even passed over the listing? Anyway, no matter how interested the customers were they would always change their minds as soon as the house went under deposit, even prior to any inspection."

"You mean the Macintoshes would keep pulling the house off the market?" I asked.

"No," replied Adam, "the customers would suddenly get cold feet and break the Macintoshes' hearts with any kind of story to get out of the deposit. One family even said 'keep the three grand; we just don't want that house!' And this went on until somebody named Tomassini bought it and uses it as a rental for college students. If you haven't introduced yourself over there yet just don't be surprised by how young they are and how soon they'll move out."

"I still don't get it", I replied. "What was changing their minds if it wasn't some structural issue found during an inspection, if they were all initially eager to buy? And how does this have anything to do with our question about Wilbur's remains?"

Adam paled and pulled back in his chair as far as the wall would permit him. He asked for a glass of water. Once that was consumed he said "Now this is only hearsay and I don't believe in such things, but the Macintoshes' realtor told me they all claimed it was haunted."

"Haunted," I nearly shouted, "a contemporary house like that haunted when we own a 250 year old house with such history having passed through these walls, how is that even plausible? Or do they think our house is haunted too?"

Adam leaned forward again. "Well no one has said anything about your house being haunted but the Macintosh property was originally part of the land that went with your place when it was the original farmstead. Maybe, some have speculated, their home was not so much haunted as was their land."

I told him it was all too much for me and I agreed with his earlier statement about not believing in such things. Still I felt disturbed. Here we were starting out trying to enjoy the fulfillment of a dream and he was telling me things that could undermine that joy and satisfaction. I would just have to pay no attention to these creepy thoughts even piled on top of poor Diamond's strange death. Adam left fairly hastily knowing his favorite clients might be leaning away from him over this news.

That evening I told Matt about my conversation with Adam repeating most of it verbatim. He laughed shaking his head; "Don't repeat any of this" he advised. "If the day ever comes when we want to sell this house, such rumors will not be an asset." I agreed but wondered how we would get more information about Wilbur. Also,

I looked at this house as our family homestead and believed we would never move. I could see our grandchildren gathered around the fireplace on a Christmas morning with their stockings all hung on the mantle. This house should be passed down through the generations, which continued to be my dream.

Once in bed that night my mind raced trying to determine what connection there could possibly be between the Macintoshes' haunting and our missing Wilbur. Just as I was about to fall asleep my eyes popped wide open, and the answer was obvious, Wilbur must be a ghost! And as I thought those words there was a thunderous crash downstairs right under our bedroom.

Matt sat bolt upright and said "What the heck was that?" We both switched on our bedside lights and grabbed our bathrobes. Clinging to each other we eased down the staircase that was nearest our room and switched on every light as we passed by. We turned the corner into our future formal living room and saw an unopened packing box lying on the floor. Nothing appeared to have fallen out of it but it was impossible to imagine how it had dislodged from its position on top of a sturdy pile of crates.

It was then we felt an extraordinary chill. The side entrance to the house was wide open and wind rushing in. I wondered how that breeze could have been strong enough to move such a heavy box; Matt said he had been wondering how I could have left that door ajar; hadn't I been jumpy already from the haunted story? We turned to each other and started shaking.

I made some chamomile tea for us from herbs I'd found in the yard. It is supposed to have a calming effect and should help us get to sleep but first we wanted to put the fallen box back in place. Matt also wanted to question me regarding the door and I wanted him to swear he had not left it open. When we had agreed that neither of us was culpable we tried to laugh but I got a little hysterical. Then we walked down the two ells checking doors and windows, checking both sides and front of the house, checking the kitchen hall door that led to the cellar and verified to each other that the house was indeed secured. Only then could we make our way back upstairs to bed; and even then we left all the lights on.

In the morning I felt groggy. Matt was already up and had the coffee going. He asked how I'd slept. I told him okay, once the lights were on. "So", he said, "You had the same dream I did then?" "Yeah, funny thing" was my reply. "Well" he rejoined, "I'll plan to get home early from the University today and have the locksmith meet me here. There is no telling just who might have a key to our doors. We probably should have had the locks changed as soon as we took ownership but the place had been vacant for so long it never occurred to me. Let's just eliminate one possibility for surprises."

"That sounds wonderful to me. I'll also see what more Priscilla may have to tell me, you know, what had she actually heard about the 'haunted house' next door. Then I'd better get some estimates on insulating the house before winter drafts cause real problems too. Cold weather is never far away in New England."

But after Matt left for work I felt overwhelmed by laziness probably due to the short night's sleep. When I stepped outside it was one of our first warm spring days and I could only think about taking a little nap in the sun. I wanted to stay next to the house in case the locksmith, Adam, or Priscilla happened by so I went to a shed and pulled out a lounge chair setting it up near the ell door. With a good book and a glass of iced tea I settled in for a little relaxation. I truly felt at peace on this beautiful property in the yard of a house which had been around nearly as long as America had been a nation.

Before I had read two pages in my novel there was another crash within the house. This time I was certain I heard glass smash so I grabbed my shoes and ran in. A painting we had hung to protect it from getting bumped while we were moving things in was hanging perilously from its peg. Glass candle sticks which had similarly been placed on a window sill to be out of harm's way were now lying on the floor, one stick shattered; while an old window shade that had come with the house had a fresh tear in it. "What is happening?"I wondered out loud.

It was then that I looked through the living room toward the kitchen and caught sight of the cellar door standing ajar. I approached it gingerly thinking of Fred's remarks about our spiders but a spider hadn't knocked a painting loose or smashed my candle holders. I tried the light switch. It was ancient, Thomas Edison likely installed it, and it was finicky, and this was the time it refused to turn things on. I got a flashlight and yelled down the stairs "Who is down there?" No one answered so I yelled again "I've got a gun so you'd better answer me and come up and explain yourself!" Still there was no reply.

"Okay", I said sternly, "I'm coming down!" And bolstered by my own words and a little prayer under my breath, I started down the rickety wooden staircase into the dark basement which was only partially illuminated by a small sooty window near the foot of the stairs, and my shaky flashlight. I continued down one foot in front of the other. My heart was thumping especially when one of the steps midway was so soft I thought my foot would go through it. I could only see shadows in front of me, the backside of the huge central chimney which was enormous gray fieldstones, a few small bottles and rags and a wooden cabinet with its door hanging partly off its hinges.

I took a step across the floor which was cement under the stairs but which I knew turned to dirt on either side of the chimney. Some latter day family had attempted to upgrade things by adding the concrete but hadn't gotten very far. The cellar walls were made of rock mostly filled in with tightly packed stone so porous that water dripped in whenever there was a heavy rain thus keeping a sump-pump very busy. There was a pronounced smell of earth and damp making me think we might grow our own mushrooms down here. Then something lightly tickled my cheek. I jumped and swung my flashlight upward as a defense weapon. I wanted to see what had touched me. It was a heavy appearing cobweb which I guess is actually a spider web with dust. There was a tremendous amount of dust in this web; maybe dust from each of the house's 250 years. I then noticed that many other webs swung from the ceiling and from the damaged cupboard. I cursed in Italian and then crossed myself.

Just as I thought 'what could make such big webs' I saw movement and beheld the terrifying Wolf Spider just standing flat against a wall. Matt is a tall man and this arachnid was the size of his two hands with the fingers spread out making a fan in two directions. The internet had not prepared me for either their enormity or their hairy appearance. I couldn't remember if they jumped or traveled in packs but I wasn't going to wait to find out. I was back up those shaky stairs and planning on running for a hairbrush to be certain I brought with me no baby spiders from the cellar!

If anything or anybody was down there with those arachnids they deserved each other was my opinion and I turned and slammed the cellar door shut and bolted the lock. The sound of the door shutting reverberated throughout the house. Suddenly a squirrel came out of nowhere heading straight for me. At first my mind didn't register what I was seeing. It distorted this rodent into a huge spider in hot pursuit. I ran from it right out the closest ell door and into the sunlight. Luck was with me as the squirrel also ran out and disappeared into a nearby oak relieving me of my terror.

A silly little squirrel had somehow gained access to the house and had run across our painting and broken the candle stick. I was really losing my grip. I turned and headed for my lounge chair for more relaxing in the sun but as I looked that way the chair was gone.

4

EXTERMINATION

It seemed a foolish thing to cry over but I was so tired and just wanted to sit in that lounge chair and enjoy my book; now the chair was inexplicably gone. I dialed Matt. I began by saying I was sorry to interrupt him at work but this idealistic, pastoral neighborhood had thieves driving by who were so pathetic that they would steal a chair right out from under me! If I hung out clothing to dry would they also take laundry right off the line?

Matt tried to calm me down. He said to remember that Adam had said we had college students living next door. Maybe taking the lounge chair was just a comic prank and they would bring it right back or maybe college kids take stuff like this. It didn't mean the neighborhood was overrun with riffraff. Then he added, "You're certain you put the chair out, right?" "Yes, of course I'm certain" I nearly snapped back obviously insulted; then I apologized for having no sense of humor.

Still, not getting much sympathy for my loss I switched gears and told him about the incident with the squirrel. My take-away-point was that we had to get the spiders under control. He said to please call the exterminator and get the spiders removed and maybe some squirrels too. It seemed like the least I could do given that he was at work and I was complaining about the lack of a lounge chair. I made the call as soon as we had rung off, got an exterminator set up for the following morning, and dashed upstairs to don street clothing. I was going to meet the neighbors.

Two sleepy looking young women answered my knock and I could see a young man on the couch behind them. He appeared to be studying with the television on. Naturally there were a few beer cans lying around as well as textbooks.

I introduced myself as the new next door neighbor. They asked me in and none of them looked in the least guilty the way I suspected a thief should. I said how nice my husband and I thought the area was and hoped that they agreed with me. I complemented their home and added they must see ours soon so they could have a sense of before and after as we tackled our project. They explained that they were only tenants while they completed their junior years at the University; adding with nervous glances at each other that they might want to try living somewhere else for next year.

I feigned complete surprise. Was there a reason they wouldn't want to stay I asked. Well said the taller of the two women, her name was Carol, there have been some strange things happening that are starting to really bother us. I encouraged her to go on and tell me more as I gently lowered myself into a chair.

"When we first moved in", Carol said, "We were always blaming each other for things that went missing or were seriously misplaced. For example I had just brought in the groceries and yet the milk was gone. Now that's a heavy item and I know it came into the house yet neither Tamisha nor Easton claimed to have seen it."

Then Tamisha interjected "the same type of thing was happening with blankets and pillows and even photographs. It was very disconcerting but then it went a step beyond."

"Yeah" added Easton from the couch, "Now it is fucking weird and spooky! For the last two nights the house's intercom turns on by itself and someone is moaning."

"Moaning?" I gasped.

"Yes, it sounds like a young male voice in a lot of pain but when we get up to look for him the system shuts down and there is no one here."

When repeating all this later to Matt over dinner he said they were likely just pulling my leg or high on something. Maybe they aren't interested in an adult neighbor popping in he mused; maybe they want to see that the relationship doesn't flourish. I made a face trying to convey my disagreement with his summation but let it go. I didn't really want to believe them either.

That night I awoke thinking I heard the moaning. Once I even shook Matt awake but he said he didn't hear a thing and rolled over away from me. A moment later he rolled back toward me. "As long as we are both awake" he began, "and we have been so busy lately" he continued in a rather seductive voice, "why don't I help you to relax?" And he offered a most charming smile. Then he gently reached for my night gown and I began helping him to pull it over my head. Although the fear of the unknown moaner might not have been 'good for the mood' Matt's beautiful smile never failed to stir me. Love making was certainly a welcome distraction. The next thing I knew it was morning and Matt was yelling up the stairs that I'd better get dressed before my exterminator showed up.

Promptly at 8:30 Peter, of Peter's Pest Services which used a hearse in their advertisements, arrived at the formal side ell door. I'm not sure why so many trades' people use the cutesy titles that they do; I suppose it is to make an impression which will stay in your mind, or separate them from other similar services, but here I was hiring Peter the bug undertaker. I described the size of our huge old spider webs to him and that I had seen at least one Wolf Spider, the size of my husband's spread hands, down in the cellar only yesterday. At that portrayal he smirked and said the body of a Wolf Spider does not extend much more than half an inch and even with sizeable legs it would not come close to a child's hand size let alone twice the circumference of my husband's. He finished with a rather macho "where are they?" which I heard as "let me at them, kid."

Then he went down the basement stairs. I elected to let him go alone but was happy for him that the lights were working again.

I'd just turned to start the tea kettle when he ran back up those stairs bursting into the hallway and shouted "Do you have a shotgun?"

"No" was my answer; "What on earth for?"

He swore that he had just seen the world's largest spider, the Goliath Bird Eater, on the wall in the cellar. "You don't understand" he had said, "These are Tarantulas from Equatorial Swamps; you've got spiders down there from the Amazon!"

"I knew they were enormous but how could that be? New England was a long distance from the Amazon!" I asked this question aloud.

"I can only conclude that someone wanted the Goliath as a pet but she didn't come alone" he stammered. "And somehow the basement was warm enough yet moist enough for them to survive and to breed."

"Breed?" I said feeling pale and not too steady; "Just how many do you think are down there?"

Peter asked for a chair and took out his cell phone. Before dialing he answered me. "I have no idea but those webs could be holding a collection of eggs. The shotgun really won't be necessary but I'm going to want my crew in here before nightfall. These things can't be left to do as they wish any longer."

At around 5 PM 'Harry the Locksmith' showed up only 24 hours late. Peter, who was now working with two other guys, suggested that Harry put his efforts off still another day as they, the bug guys, were going to be doing some serious fumigating and Harry wouldn't be safe to breathe around here until this time tomorrow. He had already warned me and Matt that we would need to leave before their work actually began and that we should not return for a full twenty-four hours. Peter said for safety reasons he should be the first one back in the house tomorrow; that he would open up doors and windows and give us a call when it was safe to return. He promised to seal the crack under the cellar door so that the gas he'd use would stay in the cellar but in order to be cautious he needed to keep us out. He inquired about pets; I responded only briefly remembering Diamond 'just the spiders' which he didn't seem to think was too funny.

I hastily packed a small bag for Matt and me. He had a favorite cousin not far away in Massachusetts who had readily invited us in for the night when we began explaining the problem. Now I tossed the valise in my car and headed to the University to pick Matt up. A pretty weird way to get to go out for dinner I thought. I also hoped, all kidding aside, that none of our 'pets' were in that bag.

When I pulled into the yard at home the next evening Peter's van was waiting for me but Peter wasn't visible. I had returned Matt to the University several hours ago because he needed to get some work done and his car was there. He expected to be home for a late meal as he was trying to make up for lost time on his research. Instead of just waiting I called Peter's cell to see when I could join him inside the house. There was no answer just a jingle about the end of days for bugs and he signed off 'Jolly Peter Rogers'. He was adding his last name to the outgoing message for more comic relief. The mailbox was full. I waited another 15 minutes and then turned the door knob closest to his van. Before I could step inside a wave of chemical smells assaulted my nose and Harry the Locksmith appeared in the driveway.

"This is when your bug guy said I could return isn't it?" he asked. "Yes," I replied "but based on how it smells in there you'd do well to swing the doors open while you change the locks." He muttered something about nobody making his job any easier but went right to his van to get things started. I put a scarf up over my nose and went inside.

I called Peter's name several times as I dashed around the house opening things up according to what he had planned to do; still no response. When I got to the cellar door, which is in a small hallway next to the kitchen, I saw that the base of this door was still packed tightly with Peter's work cloths. How strange I thought and then pulled his rags out of the way and flung the door open to dissipate more of the poison. I had been prepared to see some horrible large tarantulas' bodies scattered on the steps but what I had not anticipated was an exterminator lying face up; Peter looked dead with foam at his mouth and a greenish tinge to his skin. I screamed really loudly bringing Harry in from his locks. When he saw Peter prone just below us and looking ghastly, he grabbed me by the arm and pulled me outside. I'm glad that he did that or I might have stood there screaming for quite some time.

Coming to my senses I then hastily dialed 911. They asked questions to which I replied: "No I didn't know if the person in question was breathing; yes someone was carrying him out and giving him CPR; reason? I feared he had been poisoned and needed to breathe fresh air." The sirens began almost immediately. One good thing about this small community was that the fire stations were close-by. Matt arrived at approximately the same time and had the presence of mind to call Peter's office. We simply asked the crew to come right over, it was an emergency.

When Peter's crew arrived they were not prepared for the news we gave them. They had both worked for Peter nearly sixteen years and the worst problem they could remember was a woodchuck that kept returning to the same yard, never staying in the location to which they had relocated it, and taking less than two weeks each time it returned. They were obviously crushed by the news of his critical condition. They gave Matt their full names, addresses and phone numbers so they could go back and notify the office staff who was Peter's wife.

The first responders from the fire department had immediately called the State Troopers when they realized there was a critical injury at the scene. It seemed obvious to all that Peter had suffered a heart attack while on the job. But one thing kept nagging at me. How did the protective cloth get pushed into the crack under the door if Peter was inside the cellar?

I asked one of the officers this question. He called Harry over as though I was not a good reporter. Right in front of me he asked Harry if the cloth had still been stuffed in the door when we arrived on the scene. Harry said, "When I got here Mrs. Nelson had the cellar door open and was just standing there screaming."

"So the door wasn't jammed closed?" the officer asked. "No" was Harry's reply.

"But" I interjected "I had removed the rags and found Peter just laying there!"

"Well, it looks like we'll make our report and the doctors will have to indicate what our next step is. Don't you think in all the excitement you got confused about what you did exactly? Poor Peter must have already taken care of the door. What do you think Professor Nelson?"

Matt said he trusted me to give an accurate report but didn't think either of Peter's men would have stuffed the door shut while Peter was still down there so perhaps I was mistaken."

Matt then led me aside and, speaking quietly said, "You don't want to get either of Peter's guys in trouble do you? If a heart attack isn't the cause of this there will have to be a major inquiry especially if Peter doesn't make it. We won't get any peace around here. There will be CSI all over the property."

When he put it like that I quieted down but it did not feel honest. I simply nodded and said "I guess you are right. I must have been in shock."

That night we ended up going to a motel. The house still held the odor of poison and there would be yellow police tape around parts of the house and yard for a few days, longer if Peter didn't pull through. When would I ever get back to Wilbur?

When we settled back home the next evening something had changed for me. It wasn't the slight trace of chemicals in the air or the sadness I felt for poor Peter but knowing someone had almost died in the house took the patina off the thrill of restoration; this further dampened my spirits which were already soggy from the loss of Diamond. I'd have to stoke up my enthusiasm; perhaps talking to Priscilla about all this would help. Her antique dealer's eye made this project seem worthwhile and maybe she knew more history about the house that would rekindle my previously keen interest. After all, this had been our dream for many years.

5

JUDGMENT

Priscilla wanted to come over for tea. Understandably, the talk about Peter's accident in our house had the neighbors curious about us. I was delighted to have her visit as I could then glean more from her memory as someone who had grown up on Cemetery Hill Road. She on the other hand would be able to regale neighbors with any details I might provide her on our gruesome near tragedy; a quid pro quo.

I say near tragedy as Peter has survived. When he awoke in the hospital he told a perplexing tale of opening up the cellar door to go down the stairs and also planning to open the bulkhead door while down there. He was then intending to let air in throughout the rest of house so that his extermination spray would dissipate. It seems he was more than a little anxious to get a look at those dead Goliaths. But, he said, he had only just started down the stairs when the door closed behind him and the wedge under the door was immediately filled. Alarmed he began banging on the door assuming someone had mistakenly closed him in. After a few strong whacks and much yelling he decided to hasten down the stairs to find something to poke with under the door thus allowing some exchange of air once the rags were dislodged or to make it out the bulkhead at the far end of the cellar.

Unfortunately Peter only went a few steps when he was overcome by the remaining fumes and collapsed probably from so much heavy breathing while shouting for help. It was fortunate for him that I returned to the house a bit earlier than anticipated and thus discovered his plight. When I opened the door and roused help with my screaming I essentially saved his life. But this left yet another unanswered question: with Matt at work, Harry not yet arrived to do the locks and me coming from dropping Matt off, who had closed poor Peter in and why had they not responded to his banging and pleas for help?

The situation was still not good for Peter. He would suffer headaches for weeks due to inhaling so much of the toxic chemicals. Also his doctors had indicated the possibility of long term damage to his organs. If he would suffer organ failures, or when they might show up, was anyone's guess. Peter had been exposed to these products much of his life so that could further confound his prognosis. I guess the neighbors would have plenty to discuss. Anyway back to plans for tea with Priscilla.

By now I had improved the set up for meals with a small table and a few chairs around it. Not only did Matt and I have a place to eat but also to review contracts together as the various work estimates came in. Today I unpacked an actual tea pot and two china cups and saucers which I thought would be at the level Priscilla might expect for tea. The lack of a working stove seemed like an issue but I simply boiled water in the microwave oven which had to serve us for most of our meals. There would be no scones today however Pepperidge Farm cookies were available.

Priscilla arrived precisely at 3 and seemed excited to tell me things so that she could then ask questions. She began by saying that the first owner of the house was a judge. She explained that he had been elected as a judge in a time when most citizens were either farmers, or, if educated they were clergy; although he, this Judge Alexander Rider, had actually attained a law degree. As Judge he was expected to provide the physical location for his legal dealings and did so in what was now a front bedroom of our house. It is a large room with a fireplace and painted corner posts currently needing refurbishing.

Although he was respected, the Town's folk generally considered him harsh. He would put folks out of their meager farms if the bank complained about their mortgage being late. There was no discussion of him attempting to mediate these matters; he was cut and dried. Naturally this created bad feelings and none as bad as those between the Judge and a widow with three children. She was not able to keep the farm going after her husband was suffocated in a haying accident. Her oldest boy tried to step into his father's shoes but fell further and further behind on the mortgage payment due to the bank. When Judge Rider told them they must move in with relatives and forfeit the farm the boy snuck into the Judge's home and hanged himself somewhere. There were stories that he had done so in the Judge's chambers but others said it was in the barn or in the cellar. Priscilla said no history of the exact location was ever recorded probably due to the Judge's wishes.

"So you see," she added, "your little shock the other day was not the first untimely tragedy this house has seen." Naturally she was attempting to segue into any tidbits I might share. Under such social pressure I did confide the grim appearance of Peter when I

41

found him, which she seemed to enjoy, but I made no mention of my concern as to how Peter the exterminator had been closed into the cellar. We just both agreed how sad it was that a man so young now had an uncertain future health-wise.

Then I asked her if she had any period art work in her shop that she could see hanging on our walls? "Well" she rejoined, "my best pieces are not for sale but Walter, my handyman, is going to an auction with me next week and we will see if I spot something you might enjoy. Also by then I'll see if I can put my hands on any old photographs of your home. Those would be educational if not worthy of framing."

And as a last thought she added, "My cat has had a litter out in my antique shop. One of those kittens is just what you need for a place like this." I had never mentioned Diamond to her and certainly not that the cat had been missing or met a perplexing demise. Priscilla seemed almost clairvoyant.

As soon as the door closed behind her I wondered about the rest of her story: what the widow had done after the Judge's cruel decision resulted in her eldest child taking his own life. Perhaps Priscilla could say more another time; and did one of our rooms need an exorcism to rid it of the demons from this hanging?

The next week Priscilla called to invite me up the hill for a viewing of some art work from the auction and to choose "our kitten". The first thing I said to her was that Matt and I already owned a dog that had been staying with his parents until we had time to add a kennel onto our barn. Matt is concerned, I went on, that the two animals won't get along. Of course Diamond and Scruffy had been fast friends but I just wasn't ready for a new kitty yet.

"Oh nonsense," was her reply. "It's just a kitten and they will both simply have to adjust to new surroundings." Reluctantly I agreed to come take a look and ended up selecting a 'money cat'; so named when they are of multicolors, as I understood them to be lucky. Lord knew our house could use a little good luck.

She showed me a painting that was the portrait of a soldier in a Civil War era uniform. He was a charming looking man perhaps in his thirties with dark hair and a nice trim beard. Although this picture was more recent than I had hoped for it still held some mystique and the fellow was very handsome. Because it was unsigned she offered it at a very reasonable price and, of course she joked, the kitten is free!

As I headed for the door I reminded Priscilla that her story the previous week was not yet complete. She had included the fact that the widow in the story harbored extremely bad feelings about the Judge, understandably so, but what was the final outcome of that deep animosity? What became of the widow and her remaining children?

Priscilla sighed; "I'd hoped you wouldn't ask. It was all very unpleasant and won't cheer you regarding your property."

"Please, I insist" was my reply.

"Well nothing happened for many weeks. Really everyone in the town felt terrible for her and her family. Even the Judge showed a softening. Along with the Bank and an anonymous donor enough money was found to significantly cover her mortgage from arrears forward two full years. A number of the other farmers divided their time up so that she had free labor for at least part of every day. They took care of her crops and repairs. It was reportedly a true community effort.

"But that wasn't enough. She hated the Judge and could not move forward from the grief of losing both husband and son. It was clear to many that she wanted revenge and would be trouble. Several times the Judge's wife reported seeing her just walking past their house in the early evening, a time when she should have been home feeding her girls, but here she was a good three miles from her own place. All wondered what on earth was she doing?

"Then one morning The Rider family awakened to find a gallows like structure near their kitchen window. It didn't require much imagination to guess by whom it was erected. They took it down and used it for kindling and the Judge said not to pay any attention to it. But two days later a similar structure again appeared. This time it had a shirt belonging to the Judges oldest son wrapped around it. Now the Judge was infuriated and asked the Constable to intercede."

Suddenly Priscilla said "Goodness look at the time! I have the Board of the Historic Society coming for dinner and I have to prepare. They expect to eat old traditional fare when they dine with me so I must set a good table and be prepared to serve popovers with the roast beef. We'll talk soon." And she scurried me out the door with a painting and a kitten in tow.

6

OLD USES

Once home I made a decision not to let the past get in the way of the progress we must make to save this old relic of a house, there was still plenty of afternoon left. I'd have Matt help me name the kitten and find a place for the painting when he arrived this evening. I hoped he'd be okay with the art and the kitten too. Then I cleaned out Diamond's old litter box and set it up in the little bathroom and put a dish of water and some dry food near the kitchen fireplace. This was a rough area as the newer floor needed to be stripped down and the old hearth stone raised up but all should soon be level. The timing was perfect when Fred, our handyman, knocked on the door.

He'd heard about our trouble with the exterminator and wanted to see if we were okay and if he should get started on the kitchen floor project. Naturally I said yes but wondered if he'd first accompany me to the cellar so we could see what needed cleaning up after the fumigation. I grabbed a broom and he a bucket; what I was most pleased about was that I did not have to explore the cellar alone. At the last moment I also picked up a flashlight from the kitchen floor to be sure of decent lighting.

Well we certainly saw at least twenty large crumbly masses on the stairs, window sills and cabinet edges. These had to have once been the giant spiders' bodies. I swept them into a pile. Fred then took the broom and knocked down the huge dusty webs commenting we should probably have on masks and hats for this duty. But we were both so grimy by this point that we just kept on cleaning. As we walked around the base of the enormous stone chimney Fred began pointing things out to me.

On the north wall, next to the bulkhead, was a small square area inset from the rest of the stones, with what appeared to be a wooden shingle partially attached to it about ten inches by ten inches in size. Fred said this was "their refrigerator", and then he laughed. Actually, he explained, food was pretty much consumed as needed with the exception of things that could be pickled, cured, or dried. When it came to milk, and maybe a bit of cheese, if it wasn't eaten by night fall then the cook, probably the wife, would send someone down here to store what remained. So milk would stay cool down here which is below ground level and against these cold stones. They often had a piece of wood across the opening to further hold the cold in but after so many years the wood had all but disappeared.

I found this fascinating and much more pleasing then his next observation which was dried snake skins. There were several of these also along window sills and hanging from the support beams. Fred saw my disgusted face and laughed again, "well," he allowed, "if them snakes had really been doing their job you wouldn't have had to worry about spiders!" I made no comment wondering what the battle of snake versus Goliath would have looked like – something for my nightmares.

Then we came around to the far side of the chimney facing away from the stairs. This was the darkest part of the cellar where no tiny windows existed. Here we faced a dark entry way that appeared to go directly into the chimney although to enter this area I had to bend down as the opening was about four feet high and two feet wide. I looked at Fred who asked if I wanted him to go first. Sure I said handing him the flashlight.

Again a laugh: "Come on in," he chuckled. I entered having no idea what to expect. We seemed to be in a little room surrounded on all sides by stones. It was wide enough for a card table and could have accommodated four or so six year olds to play around in the remaining space. What was this I asked totally at a loss for an explanation; were they part of the Underground Railroad?

"No", was Fred's answer. "Have you noticed a brick missin' up high on the back wall inside your big kitchen fireplace?"

"Yes, it seems to have fallen out but the rest of the bricks are firm so we weren't worried and it is well below the roof."

"Well," Fred continued, "That stone was intentionally left out, it wasn't damaged - it never existed. The idea was that these farmers all had to survive by taking care of their own selves. This hole helped 'em in soap making which was necessary for use with the cattle, laundry and hand washin'. They waited until a fire had died down and when it was nothin' but a large pile of cold ashes it was shoveled down that hole. It took a lot of ash to make large flats of soap so they would shovel it in for many weeks before enough would be collected. "

"The ash needed a room of its own but it also needed to be self-contained so the rest of the house wouldn't get sooty. And having a little stone chamber surrounded by the chimney had a second advantage just in case the ash still contained a live ember. Also there was the matter of actually making the soap which involved using purified fat, lye, and ammonia with some other harsh chemicals. This was nothin' you wanted your kids gettin' into. There were enough farmin' and cookin' accidents in them days that you didn't want to add fallin' into a vat of liquid soap to the list."

I thanked Fred for all this information. It was fascinating. Perhaps one day our guests would use soap which we had actually produced ourselves. I'd just have to learn how to color it and to produce a sweet smell. Something we'd consider for another time.

We went back upstairs. Fred said he'd begin his measurements for leveling the floor and see what materials needed ordering. I planned to call the company that said they could blow insulation into the walls or explain other ways to insulate the house; and also to get an estimate on having the roof redone. Certainly Matt would relish a report filled with progress: now what to make for supper?

With lasagna baking in the newly delivered oven, which was at least temporarily installed, and a salad started, I began to think about names for the kitten. Matt actually seemed delighted when he met the sweet little cat and he was even more enthusiastic about the painting of the soldier. He pronounced the cat was to be called Sybil, after a famous case of a multiple personality disorder as that was what his latest research was examining. I cringed a little fearing his study was a bit passé but Matt had defended this decision believing that the subject had been let go of far too soon by the world of psychology. He believed he'd uncover some important work and I certainly wanted him fulfilled. It was as though he had an almost personal agenda with this topic. Something else we'd discuss when things settled down.

I was the product of an Italian mother and an American/Anglo father. My mother had been born to an Italian girl whose parents never wed. All she could say about her dad was that he had been an Italian man who was a US citizen serving in World War II. Apparently my Nonna thought it was love but the soldier left with the troops and never contacted her again even though she had told him she was pregnant. My Nonna had felt disgraced but the situation wasn't all that uncommon. Her parents accepted her with the baby and life went on.

That baby was to become my mother and she was raised to be fiercely independent and to achieve in academics which was just starting to be accepted for Italian women. While studying at the University of Rome she met a handsome, blonde and charming American exchange student who had an English and German background. He loved her and wanted to get married. Given the circumstances of her birth she was very pleased by this. However, she did not want to leave Italy for more than a visit; would he relocate to Rome she asked? Crazy in love he said yes and the wedding took place on a hillside under grapevines at outside tables. I was to be the only product of that relationship. After about three years my dad couldn't handle his expatriate status. They divorced (Italy now permitted this) with me becoming a transatlantic child. I got my education in Italy and dad would visit at Christmas time and occasionally as his job permitted. I would then spend every summer on Cape Cod where my American grandparents lived and Dad would be there every weekend.

It was a bit unusual but we all managed because it was amicable. My parents still loved each other but couldn't live in the other's country. I profited from learning two languages as a native speaker and, of course, two cultures. When it was time for college I found it more beneficial to be admitted into an American University as the Italian system was more competitive and perhaps overly influenced by politics. The questions on the national examination were structured so that politics might be involved with some students getting advanced information about the examination: that is at least what my Italian friends and cousins told me. Whatever it was I wanted a straight forward way to gain university entry and America has so many universities. Interestingly enough, at that time, my mother moved to the States saying "it was temporary"; I guess she still wanted to be near me. Now she is living with my dad.

As a person with dual citizenship I was welcomed to Brown Universality after completing specific examinations and qualifications. This is where I eventually met Matt. Rhode Island is also a state with a large Italian population making me feel more at home and I could easily get real Italian style calamari.

From time to time my mother had mentioned that she was a witch. Now every kid thinks that of their mother on occasion but this is from a different context. My mother would tell me someone I had just brought home was about to receive bad news or would soon be notified of a serious illness or a death in the family. Of course these are vague enough to fit many possibilities but her ability to be correct was uncanny. "Laura's mother" would suddenly have a stroke at a very early age or "Gina" would say her father just lost his job and they had to move away; all things within the realm of possibility but very improbable when within a few weeks of my mother's pronouncements. She was best at knowing when someone was a "phony". I think she was very sensitive to sincerity or the lack thereof. She could say "that boy is cheating on your friend Julia" and in a short time his peccadilloes would come to light.

This gave mother a little more power over me as I was always in fear that she would make such a prediction aimed my way. When I got to college I began to have these "witchy" feelings myself. It started innocently enough when I was pretending to read cards and tell the futures of my dorm mates. Invariably I would say something that made them gasp or ask pointedly "How could you know that?" I didn't know how I knew it, the message or feeling just came to me. But I also took care to be vague enough that I only needed to catch an edge of their reality to look astute. There were certainly people who fooled me.

Matt had only met my mother once before the wedding. She said "He seems like a nice young man." This didn't sound like a resounding endorsement but she didn't caution me to "run fast" either. Naturally we went to Rome for our honeymoon and mother warmed to Matt just knowing he loved Italy. Matt had liked my spontaneity and my intelligence; I had been drawn not only to his looks but a sense of stability. What I wanted from a marriage was two people who could love each other and live on the same continent; and as I have mentioned we hoped a family would be part of this along with the perfect house.

Matt taught most days, advised students and worked with his graduate students to produce and refine studies worthy of publication. Some research belonged primarily to the students with Matt guiding them to avoid errors and to follow research methodology. Some graduate students received stipends to work under Matt on studies he designed and would publish with his name as first author. The students would be considered as secondary authors receiving recognition, learning the intricacies of publishing and they would be able to list these studies on their curriculum vitae. This pursuit was really an endless job for someone as ambitious as Matt and at a time when the final decision of tenure was about to be made. He needed the multiple personality disorder study to be published in a top tier journal and to be quoted by his colleagues. He further needed to get other details of that same study published in other well respected journals. This would highlight the point that he had earned a national reputation and would be granted lifelong employment by the University of Connecticut. Failure to achieve this, the denial of tenure, meant the faculty member would need to find a new employer and somehow the fate of having been "denied tenure" would follow him or her like the Scarlet Letter, a disgrace.

Knowing this made me want to do all I could to simplify Matt's home life. I'd keep managing the repairs and renovations and preparing the meals so that Matt could remain dedicated to his research even when he had to go back to the University after dinner to meet with students or to run data. This is also why I wanted to let some of the mystery hunting go. We could find out more about Wilbur, what had really happened to Diamond, who had left the Goliath spiders in our cellar and what had the Judge's enemy conjured on him, once the house was in better shape and Matt had achieved tenure. That was my plan anyway until two days after Sybil came to live with us. I had vowed not to let her out, to simply keep her safe and well fed in the kitchen. But that morning we came downstairs and Sybil was gone; utterly and completely gone.

7

SPLIT PERSONALITY

My reaction to the missing kitten was way out of proportion. I simply became hysterical immediately assuming she would be dead on the street or in the mouth of whatever creature had delivered Diamond's corpse to the back door. She must have snuck out when we didn't see it, perhaps the last time Matt got home from work. I made him drive down the street and see if she was by the side of the road. Meanwhile I ran out in back of the house still in my nightgown and flip-flops. I screamed "here kitty-kitty" as I was certain she had not yet learned the name Sybil.

When Matt pulled back up the driveway I too gave up and we went into the house. He said although he had not found her that was really good news because that meant she had not been run over. I gave an exasperated sigh and said poor little kitty. That was when we heard it. There was a plaintive mewing sounding like it came from the top of the cellar stairs. I rushed to the door and threw it open. A very bedraggled looking kitten stood there crying. She was frightened and hungry no doubt, perhaps having been down there all night. She rubbed on us each and then went to her box. What a good girl.

While we were feeding and petting her we kept discussing how she had ended up down in the basement: neither one of us had gone down there all evening; nor could anyone remember even stepping into that cellar! Suddenly I looked up at the missing brick in the chimney where previous owners had shoveled down their ashes. I turned to Matt and asked if he thought a kitten could jump that high; and indeed he did. She must have been curious about the hole and ended up taking a long flight onto the floor below. It is amazing she was so pliable that the fall didn't hurt her. We'd have to place something over that opening at least until she was bigger or we needed to light a fire. One mystery solved.

Matt grabbed some toast with peanut butter and headed to the University. He and his key graduate students were taping interviews this morning of people that either believed they had multiple personality disorders or who had actually been diagnosed as such. The researchers would then select specific criteria which either supported or detracted from their claims. In at least two cases the folks diagnosed with the disorder denied that it was true. Interesting since I understood part of the problem was often that the patient did not know of his or her other identities.

I found that a fascinating thought as I prepared for a consultation with the insulation team to be followed by a visit to a kitchen supply warehouse. At the warehouse I would select samples to at least run by Matt so we would both enjoy the kitchen cabinets and counters. We really had to do almost everything from scratch; a fact that had been highlighted the first night in the home when we flushed the upstairs toilet and then discovered it had dripped down the dining room wall. Yuck!

It was a relief to know that Matt would be eating his dinner at work. He needed more time for analysis and I needed more time for the house. Maybe I could even fit in a visit to the oldest church, which was located in the center of town, to see if it held any old death records or certificates. I couldn't completely give up on Wilbur after all.

Arriving at the church I was struck by just how old it looked up close. It had to be even older than our place and I did recall reading that the first thing these settlers did was to build a common building for shelter. Later they converted it to the church when their individual farms had been constructed. Laboring in common they achieved more and there was safety in numbers in terms of possible attacks by the native peoples. The church still bore cedar shakes and shingles paying homage to those early settlers. The steeple was not as high as many more recent places of worship and it matched the shutters in terms of a handmade quality and simplicity.

However, by this time of day the pastor was just locking up and suggested I look around the grounds. A few stones were located on the property, in gardens and as plaques on benches as memorials set up by the families. Although they didn't mark the sites of any bodies they might contain valuable information. I thanked him and began a walk around the building keeping my eyes open for any more snakes. A short time later I found something very interesting; in fact, so interesting that I decided to immediately share this find with Matt even though he was at his office.

When I arrived on campus it was late enough that the parking restrictions were lifted until the next morning. I got very close to Matt's building and parked next to his car. I knew the lower door near his laboratory was generally unlocked for easy student access and went in that route. Almost immediately I could hear Matt's voice. Not only was he speaking loudly, he was shouting and angry. I walked toward his lab without detection as no one would hear me over the brouhaha he was creating. Matt was berating a student for apparently giving a little too much information to a participant. He was saying "Yes, of course there is informed consent but you contaminated everything this subject can tell us by letting her know what outcome we anticipate. This will never be regarded as objective!"

This evaluation from the faculty member would have been difficult enough for the student to hear but now he was being told by Matt, in front of other students, that he was an idiot and had no business in graduate school! "Holy smokes is this my husband talking?" I asked myself. The young man kept apologizing but Matt never let up so I finally decided to make my presence known. If Matt yelled at me I'd deal with him later but this kid needed an intervention!

When Matt saw me in the doorway his entire affect changed. He became calm and, lowered his voice and smiled at his assistant. He started explaining in almost gentle terms that there had been a major error although certainly not insurmountable; something that would be a growth experience for the whole team. He then gave the class a break just before introducing me to everyone. The students seemed anxious to get some air so I soon had Matt to myself.

I felt I had to address what I had observed but was careful not to challenge Matt. Then I explained that since the group was having some difficulties maybe my story could wait until later but he insisted that he wanted to know right then. I explained about visiting the Church and said there had been a plaque posted honoring a Reverend Wilbur who had served the community for twenty years from 1809 to 1829 which included the dates of "our" Wilbur's birth and death. Wilbur must be a surname and his dad must have been this clergyman.

Matt said that was a great find and understood why I had been so excited. He would like to consider it for awhile and we could discuss it later. He felt he must get back to his students but kissed my cheek and told me to drive carefully. I left very much regretting what I had witnessed while at the same time being filled with a sense that I would profit from what had been learned here tonight and I did not mean at the church.

Was my sweet husband capable of being a tyrant in the classroom? Did I simply see him on an off night while he was under too much stress or was his modus operendi to rule by force and control and behave in a punitive manner if something went wrong? I was confused. If that was who he was why had I not seen it before?

I fell asleep before Matt returned home and while I slept I dreamt of Matt, although in my dream he was Judge Rider, harsh, respected and later hated. He was good to me as long as I did his bidding but once I stepped out of line he would actually crack a horse whip across my backside – anywhere that would not show in public. I awoke drenched in sweat.

In the morning Matt seemed his usual self. He made no mention of the student incident but asked what I thought regarding the "Wilbur Family". I, on the other hand, wasn't thinking of much other than the fact I was filled with a sense that we had lived in this house before.

8

THE OLD TESTAMENT

Now I was really being ridiculous. I did not believe in the supernatural or the occult; but did I believe in the Holy Ghost and the Resurrection? I wasn't truly clairvoyant, that would be my mother. I was only able to pull off stupid party tricks with very gullible college girlfriends. I needed to concentrate on my real world duties. Fred was planning to bring other carpenters over today and we'd make decisions about strengthening floors and how many windows we could afford to replace this year. Also it was time to get the plumber and electrician in ahead of any finish work; and given the age of the house I'd better get the chimney inspected before we lit any fires.

Fred took care of a great deal really acting as our general contractor. By the time jobs were agreed upon it was getting late enough that I hastened to call the Pastor before he was again gone from the church. I wanted to know what records they had of Reverend Wilbur. I caught him at a good time and he asked if I'd come over so he could provide me with some reading material on "the Rev. Wilbur years" he phrased it. I was off on the short drive to the church.

Pastor Martin told me that Rev. Wilbur was not the founder of the church for that had happened from the earliest times of the Town and the congregation had been small with just a few families making up its 120 or so members; but when Rev. Wilbur came to the area in 1809 he had been the first fulltime pastor the church people could afford to employ. He had arrived with a box of bibles, a few furnishings, a wife and 3 little girls. Word had been given to him in Boston that there was a church in need of a clergyman so he had purchased a wagon and come to "fulfill his destiny" as he described it.

Prior to his arrival the church had been served by deacons elected by the congregation to handle the business of the church. Most matters were cared for by committees the Deacon chaired. There was a building and grounds committee, a tithing committee, a charities committee, general maintenance, and special services. Special services included baptisms, weddings and funerals plus the occasional decorating of the altar as gardens and inclinations allowed. The congregation worked as a team to see that all these needs were met. There was a sense of pride through the investment of time and effort fostering the cause of their bond.

But as more families came to the area and the agricultural school was forming nearby, it became more necessary for a pastor to be hired to meet the daily needs of the community. And if the truth is told as more people joined the church there were also minor disagreements that might occur even over such trivial things as who would clean up after flowers were brought in or competition over who had raised the most beautiful blooms and given these to the church, not pridefully but out of love. It was hoped a fulltime minister could squelch such fussing before any lasting animosity occurred.

When Rev. Wilbur appeared he seemed to be just what folks had wanted. He was a good looking man about 35 with light brown hair, blue eyes and skin dark enough that it appeared he was used to physical labor as well as academic. He presented Deacon Brown with a certificate in Theology from a Boston School, politely introduced a sweet although somewhat plain looking woman as his wife and pointed to each girl naming them as Genesis, whom they called Ginny, Leviticus, called Levy, and Esther. Then he joked that they would name their last child "Exodus" which drew embarrassed smiles from the Deacon and the few congregants present.

Deacon Brown then introduced the Reverend and his family to Emily Harrison who had been the volunteer secretary to the church for many years. It was she who kept the church records recording all the special events of births, deaths and marriages. Emily also had a private file the others knew nothing about. She thought of it as sort of the Church's Diary. In it she listed the names of those who asked for special charitable help, how much they received and did they ever pay it back or simply keep asking for more. She told herself these notes contained no value judgments but believed there should be a reckoning somewhere. She also kept track of those individuals who seemed to make frequent demands on the Deacon's time; who couldn't solve their own problems or needed the Deacon to summon help for them with their farm management. She saw this latter group as somewhat weak or too needy. Without being asked she would occasionally remind these families to turn to God when need arose and to offer help in return to the Church. Most members preferred not to deal with Miss Emily but she was an immense help to the Deacon. She also had the advantage of being unattractive; her nose was pointed a bit, her hair was rather lack luster, and her large teeth not only protruded but were set above a small chin. Truth-be-known a few of the children in the parish secretly called her "Whinny" and made sounds like a horse when she passed by.

The advantages of this appearance were that it kept tongues from wagging and caused no discomfort for the Deacon's wife. Her lack of outer beauty also insured her availability as she had no family to attend to and was unlikely to have such prospects. The Deacon did not foresee that her personal time might one day be filled with unchristian as well as Godly deeds.

Knowing her value to the congregants Deacon Brown proposed to Rev. Wilbur that he would be well served to keep her on as secretary and offer her a small wage. Rev. Wilbur replied to this in the affirmative and Emily graciously accepted the offer. Pastor Martin was now offering me the Church Diary beginning with Rev. Wilbur's first Sunday as written and maintained by Miss Emily Harrison. Then he handed me a second folder which contained a personal diary he had only recently obtained, also written by Miss Harrison.

Sunday, June 13, 1809 Congregational Church of East Apple, Connecticut

Rev. Wilbur arrived at 6:30 AM in preparation for his 9:00 AM service. He had wished to begin services earlier allowing for more home tyme for the congregation after church but as some had to walk here it was recommended to him by Deacon Brown that 9 would be the earliest possible for most. He seemed to accept this and strife was avoided. His sermon consisted of an introduction of himself and family and then a reading from the Song of Solomon:

> *"The winter is past,*
> *the rain is over and gone.*
> *The flowers appear on the earth,*
> *the time of singing has come" (Song 2.11, 12)*

He followed this by saying his arrival and God's endless love would be a new beginning for this church and every family within it. Literally we were entering summer and he would feed the parishioners' souls so that we might bloom along with the Lord's flowers. He added that we could put our trust and faith in him, meaning the Reverend, as well as in the Lord; for which he received a resounding AMEN. All seemed smitten with the dear man. Plans were made for a supper the following Saturday night, to be held at the Church, so that all could celebrate. The families assembled would bring the food. A sign-up sheet for the meal was passed around. Addie was known for her baked beans, Susan and Hattie Reynolds for their deep dish apple pie and molasses cookies, and the Rogers for their pork stew while Mrs. Smyth made trays of delicious relishes: we left delighted and energized.

On a weekly basis Miss Harrison gave similar reports for many weeks. Things were positive and glowing and filled with praise for how The Reverend Wilbur comforted the grieving, mediated difficulties within families and rejoiced with those becoming married and having babies and Baptisms. He gave of his time freely and happily and never seemed to weary of caring for his flock. Then something appeared to be changing.

September 1, 1809 Church Office

Reverend Wilbur has made numerous journeys to the home of Mrs. Alice Bridgefield. Mrs. Bridgefield had lost her husband in a farming accident approximately two years prior to the Reverend's arrival. Her brother and his family had relocated here to take over the farm and to live with Alice. She seemed to be well on her way to recovery from the tragedy when Rev. Wilbur arrived. She must have then slipped into a delayed depression or been having a serious crisis of faith after she got to know the Reverend. His attention was being required on a weekly basis. Perhaps he reminded her of her late husband and that is what was upsetting her. I only know that every Sunday he receives a note from her requesting that he stop-bye.

Here on I refer only to her private diary for that tells the real story.

September 8, 1809

It happened again today. During the recessional Mrs. Bridgefield reached out and tucked something into the Reverend's sleeve. I don't think either one of them thought it was noticed but I for one saw the entire thing. This may become unseemly. I shall have to counsel the Reverend that for the sake of the congregation he must put the needs of other members ahead of this widow.

Post note: I caught up to The Reverend after all had left the service and told him in no uncertain terms that this much attention to one widow, although undoubtedly kind of him, was going to look bad. He was surprised but thanked me for pointing this out and said he would take care of Mrs. Bridgefield that I should not worry about him or the Church any further. We shall see.

September 29, 1809

It has been three weeks and Rev. Wilbur seems to have been good at his word. He has been busy on these premises or accounted for his tyme well with other families. Perhaps I was too suspicious.

January 9, 1810

There was a Ladies Fellowship Tea this afternoon in our building. Mrs. Wilbur, who never says two words, she is quite introverted which is often the case with wives of talkative men, wanted to speak with me privately before the Reverend returned with the buggy to pick her up. It seems she is worried that he is working too hard, rarely spends the evening meal with them and wondered how I might think of a way he could lighten his load. I was shocked but kept that from her. Indeed, why is he not home for his supper? At any rate I told her that I would give it some thought.

January 30, 1810

We've just returned to the Church after 10 days of blocked roads and overwhelmed horses. The Reverend does not look well. He tells me he was late getting home during the blizzard as he was caught at a parishioner's. Perhaps "caught" is the true meaning of what he is confiding. But when I ask for clarification he only says "there is no problem only that Mrs. Wilbur was anxious." I daresay she was. And I wonder what Mrs. Bridgefield's brother could be thinking about this although he has never set foot in the Church so I am unlikely to find out.

February 28, 1810

I must report no mention of Mrs. Bridgefield nor has she returned to Church. The Reverend has seemed out of sorts and a bit short tempered but he is here every day. Sometimes Mrs. W makes his lunch and brings it over. She has even asked me to join them although I never would. God must have performed a miracle; I really thought they were headed for trouble.

June 30, 1810

As Secretary I was attending the Building and Grounds meeting sitting beside the Reverend. During a break Mrs. Alabaster stuck her head between us, she standing, leaning close to the Reverend and in what struck my ear as a loud whisper (I think they call it a stage whisper) asked if the Reverend had seen Mrs. Bridgefield recently. He seemed a bit dismayed that she would be asking him this question but replied "Why no." Her rejoinder was that she feared the poor widow was in some trouble. The Alabasters had happened by the farm intending to buy eggs and noticed Mrs. Bridgefield must be six months with child and her husband already in the ground for several years!

I pretended to be concentrating on my notes but naturally I was listening. My head immediately went back to the occasion of the blizzard. Would that not be six months past?

The Reverend stammered a bit then said he was sure there must be some innocent explanation. Did Mrs. Alabaster know that some ailments created a bloating of the gut? Perhaps poor Mrs. Bridgefield was unwell. Perhaps this accounted for her long absence from Church. He would certainly make it his business to pay a call on Mrs. Bridgefield and her dear brother Edwin Thompson. Perhaps the Church could be of help to them. He was only sorry he had not thought to visit them sooner and thanked Mrs. Alabaster profusely for bringing the matter to his attention.

Reverend Wilbur seemed unsettled for the remainder of the meeting. At its conclusion he informed me he'd be into the Church Office later in the day tomorrow as he had some urgent business to which he must attend in the morning. I accepted this thinking I couldn't wait to hear the story upon his return. I frankly had no use for Mrs. Alabaster as she never seemed kindly disposed toward anyone. If there were two ways to look at a situation she saw what the horse left on the ground. I always thought it was because her husband was struggling to make a living as a lawyer by traveling around the area and she spent her time baking or asking people for books to place on loan in her shed. She fancied herself a librarian but I doubt that she had read much. I think the most exciting thing that ever happened to her was when she cracked an egg and found two yolks. Naturally she needed the business of others' for a little stimulation.

July 2, 1810

8 AM: I never saw the Reverend yesterday but he was here when I arrived this morning. He doesn't seem to be in a very good mood and has made no mention of what he was up to. I shall have to wait.

10 AM: I can wait no more; surely he needs someone in whom to confide. I asked him how he found Mrs. Bridgefield, was she well? He appeared to struggle to brighten-up but then he pulled himself together, likely for my sake. He sat up straighter in his chair, softened his expression and even smiled. "Why yes", he said. "She was very well and pleased that the church folks were thinking of them. She was also excited to report that her sister-in-law is having a baby in a few months and perhaps they will desire a proper Christening even though her brother is generally not very Godly. She has asked me to return to their farm soon for further discussion with the whole family. Now isn't that grand? We will retain and gain members of the congregation!" Hump, I thought, while outwardly smiling, so that is how he will account for his love-child. I said no more.

July 3, 1810

4 PM: He has not shown himself today and left no note of explanation. Perhaps I shall soon need eggs from the Bridgefield farm for a special project; my three hens may not produce enough. In any case tomorrow is the 4ᵗʰ of July so no one will be in the office but the entire town will turn out on the green at some point. The old cannon will be fired and families will be picnicking. Sam Loomis will play his fife and Harold Smyth will beat on his drums and I for one shall be glad when that racket has ended.

July 5, 1810

5 PM: I stopped into the office to retrieve my knitting bag. To break-up many work days I often do a bit of crocheting for about 10 minutes just to reward myself but realized the bag had not come home with me. I wished to sit on the porch and do a bit of needle work this evening. But much to my amazement the poor Reverend was sitting there holding his head and sobbing to the point where he must not have heard me enter the room! I stopped immediately and begged his pardon for the intrusion, explaining hastily why I was there. He turned to me with soulful eyes, his entire countenance wet and chin quivering, and said "Dear Emily whatever am I to do?" Then he resumed sobbing like a grief-stricken child.

I was so surprised and filled with a warmth which I can only imagine as maternal for he had never even used my given name before, that I rushed to his side and pulled him into my arms and proceeded to comfort him by patting his back and saying; "There, there, what on earth has happened to upset you so my dear friend? How may I help you?"

After a tyme he was able to speak and told me he must beg me to be confidential for he had no one else to whom he could turn. It seems that Mrs. Bridgefield is with child, and here he broke down again saying, I was the only one to whom he could turn. It seems when he went out to her farm on July 1 he discovered the truth just by looking at her. He described her mood as both tense and joyful: She had always wanted to have children but had all but given up when she became a widow. The *reality of a baby arriving was thrilling to her but the circumstances of having it be born out of wedlock horrified her.*

It was then that Rev. Wilbur, hoping to ease her pain, suggested that her sister-in-law lead people to believe that she is pregnant and Mrs. Bridgefield would outwardly play the role of a dear auntie once the child is born. She seemed content with that and much more at ease but when the Reverend left she was again overwhelmed by her own demons. What if she didn't like sharing the parenting with her sister-in-law? What if the town guessed at the truth and the child's life was made miserable? Would the child be raised in a lie? And how was she to afford this mouth to feed unless the father stepped forward?

At this point I thought to put the poor Reverend out of his misery. If he wanted me as his confidant then I needed to know the whole story. So I stated the obvious: "And you, even though a man of God and a married man with three children, had a moment of weakness and are the responsible party?"

He looked away from me and I feared he would not answer but he began crying again and said "Yes, God forgive me, yes!" I held him again and then began to feel stirrings deep within me that I had not experienced in years. I could help the Reverend Wilbur but perhaps I would occasionally need a little something myself.

Thus we spent the next several hours talking, planning and comforting each other. I told him it would be possible for me to skim just a little money off the weekly donations and put it aside for the care of the child. That I was the only one who truly knew what was taken in when cash was placed in the collection plates and the Treasurer based his report upon what I recorded. A few congregants made pledges and I would not be able to "short" those or there could be demands to see my records. Most of these pledges came from those who truly tithed but there were only a few of these folks. More likely we would receive donations at the backdoor from those with no money. They would leave a sack of potatoes, a basket of eggs, tomatoes or apples and other fruit; sometimes they would leave fresh pies and even hard cider. What the Reverend's family couldn't use we always gave to the poor. In some cases I daresay we returned goods to the very folks who had left them at the church! I would just set aside whatever food might help Mrs. Bridgefield and the babe and the Reverend could take it along to them.

He seemed reconciled to this strategy and planned to discuss it with Mrs. Bridgefield the next day. Before he left he kissed me on the mouth. This was the best fireworks I had ever experienced. Then he clung to me for a moment and left.

9

A SCHEME

Miss Emily Harrison continues below. Just to remind the reader I have left out many of her entries which are strictly church business and accountings not related to the situation with Rev. Benjamin Wilbur, Mrs. Alice Bridgefield, the baby, and herself and I am only sharing her <u>private</u> diary.

July 8, 1810

7:30 PM: Rev. Wilbur has just left for the short ride to his home from which he has been away since daybreak. He has had another visit with Mrs. Bridgefield and reports, with great relief that we are now all in agreement. His first proposal to her had been that she implore her sister-in-law to pretend to be the mother of this baby-to-be. That he and the Church would handle all financial responsibilities and whenever possible he would assist her brother in the farming chores. In exchange none of them would ever mention that Mrs. B was actually the baby's mother and there would be no need to mention paternity. Mrs. B rejected this proposal once again. She wanted her "daughter", she said, to know her true mother and to have a loving relationship based on truth.

It was impossible for the Reverend to argue with this. His second proposal was that she would state the true matter of being the girl's mother and he would see that Church Death Records were altered enough such that the late Mr. Bridgefield could have fathered this child and then passed away almost immediately; thus making the girl legitimately a Bridgefield. But then Mrs. B's brother pointed out the deed to the farm had already been altered to contain his name and he did not want that changed.

Finally it was agreed that Mrs. B would reluctantly and sadly admit to a few Church ladies that while her brother had been out working in the pasture, and his wife was milking the cows, she had let a stranger who was walking along their road come in for a glass of milk. They had plenty of milk and it seemed the Christian thing to do as he appeared poor and hungry. In fact she would have sent him along with bread and cheese but once his thirst was quenched he grabbed her pushing her down on the kitchen floor and raped her right there!

She had been mortified and was barely able to tell her brother what had occurred. The culprit was long gone by the time she explained what had happened and then they were all in the middle of the first snow of the season which turned out to be the horrendous blizzard. She liked this story even though it would be difficult to tell the child, should she have to one day, who her father was. However, as it protected the Reverend, his family and his job he decided to agree to it. He and the Church would do all they could for her.

And so the waiting began and the next day I commenced to find ways of specifically supporting that family.

September 25, 1810

8 PM: All had been going along smoothly. Rev. Wilbur was as attentive to Mrs. Wilbur and his girls as he could possibly manage while helping to placate Mrs. B and relying on me to take care of the financial matters. Naturally he showed me his gratitude in a loving way and I was thrilled by every touch, pat or kiss I received. My appearance had been made fun of all of my life. My own father had said the family thought me sweet-looking and loved me but there was no dowry large enough to overcome the unfortunate hand God had dealt my face; yet I was bright and hardworking and my folks made certain I could inherit their property and at least not have to rely upon a man to support me. I never expected to experience romance and so I simply felt blessed each day that the Reverend turned to me.

Then we received word at 4 PM: Mrs. B had been in labor all night and had just given birth to a healthy son but she had lost a lot of blood. The midwife was concerned and had sent for a medical doctor. Rev. Wilbur left for their farm immediately. Later, on his way home, he stopped by the Church when he saw my buggy still tethered there. He was again in dire straits.

Mrs. B had suffered a seizure of some sort and had died before the doctor arrived. He and the midwife had held her hands as she uttered her last words. She said something about "Wilbur" which the midwife took to mean that the baby should be named Wilbur not that Mrs. B was addressing the Reverend with her last breath. Rev. Wilbur was filled with turmoil ranging from guilt to horror to love and then guilt again. He had wanted a son but certainly not this way; but of course, this was his son.

I asked how Mr. Thompson had reacted to all this with his sister's loss and a new baby in the house? Ben, as I sometimes called him when we were alone, seemed to answer from a deep haze. He said at first Edwin had acted angry but his wife seemed to settle him down. Ben was fearful Edwin would blame him completely for the entire tragic mess. But the wife's counsel must have reminded him of what they had to gain. For example, the entire farm would now be theirs except for one factor that no one had counted on when Mrs. Bridgefield's Will was drawn up. She now had a surviving male heir.

The Reverend continued that he hastily told them he would take the child and adopt him and remove that issue if the Thompsons did not want their nephew. Little more was said as the midwife was still present. Mr. Thompson walked the Reverend out to his buggy. It was then that the gentlemen decided the Reverend would come back for the boy after he had an opportunity to discuss it with Mrs. Wilbur. Mrs. Thompson and the midwife would care for the infant that night.

Apparently Mr. Thompson wanted nothing more to do with the entire situation and said there would be no need for the Church to support his family so long as the Reverend took the child. Ben said it was difficult to keep his grief from too obviously turning into joy. When he saw I was still at the Church he could not wait to tell me. But, he was uncertain as to how Mrs. Wilbur would receive the news.

I grabbed his arm and held it fast. "Could I raise this child?" I asked; adding "With you, here in the Church except at night when he would sleep in his own bed in my home?" The Reverend said "That might work, let me sleep on it and ask the Lord's guidance."

September 26, 1810, 8 AM

Rev. Wilbur looked as though he had not slept well. He sat down beside me and explained he had harbored selfish thoughts. He had thought to pass as the boy's true father by raising the baby within his home with his three daughters. To that end he had beseeched Mrs. Wilbur to open her heart to the poor orphaned child so that he might bring him home. But he was shocked that the very suggestion of such a thing had resulted in a most violent reaction erupting from his usually quiet wife. He quoted her as saying "I'll not have that bastard set foot in our home!" Obviously she left no chance for negotiation.

And so he was confessing all this to me by way of saying "Yes, we shall raise the boy together primarily in the Church but he will be your son and legally live at your home." And, he added, "I am a fortunate man to have you by my side in this and all things of late. You know me better than does any other."

I am but a plain looking 43 year old spinster. In a very short period of time I have become involved with a handsome well educated man easily ten years my junior and will now raise his baby. It is almost too much to accept but I am extremely grateful. God moves in mysterious ways. And later this morning Rev. Wilbur and I will ride out together on our mission of mercy where I will return holding the tiny baby boy.

10

A BRILLIANT SON

What followed in the notes I received from Pastor Martin were many pleasant although mundane details of raising a child. Miss Emily always spoke lovingly of the boy and Reverend Wilbur. They seemed to make a real family by day, and she was content with just the child, in the evenings when Benjamin was home with his wife and other children. The congregation appeared to accept the arrangement and the story that they told. There were only a few derogatory words coming from Mrs. Alabaster to whom no one paid much attention. In fact several families brought their children around the church just to play with young "Will" as he grew older. Also Miss Emily received prepared food items and slightly used infant clothing when the situation was first announced to the Church.

Additionally Miss Emily Harrison made Wilbur Harrison her heir with the Reverend as executor of her estate. It was unusual for a woman to own the large home she had and all the farmland so she was certainly making it legal that it be passed on to "their son" as she thought of young Will. Occasionally she made reference to the passion she and the Reverend felt, or surprise at the ecstasy "they shared," but she gave no details. Mrs. Wilbur was rarely mentioned and then only to recall some annoyance she had caused by demanding time from the Reverend that should have gone to Wilbur. Still it seemed the "Mrs." left them pretty much alone.

Much of the early years for Will were noted as one would see in a baby book: when he first rolled over, his first tooth, first steps, etc. She also was delighted in teaching him to say "Mama" and then more carefully he was coached to say "Reverend Ben" which were difficult words for a little one. Will also proved to be a very intelligent little fellow easily learning colors; animal sounds, the alphabet and then reading and arithmetic. Soon they agreed to send him to the small neighboring school house for a few hours a week. Here he delighted in playing with other children and was quickly being promoted through the grades.

His father took over more of Will's education as it became apparent just how gifted he was. They read the bible and wrote stories about Jesus, took many walks in the woods collecting specimens and detailing the anatomy of any creature whose bones they might happen upon. Miss Emily sent away for books with information and pictures of exotic animals so that Will also knew about zebras, giraffes and elephants. It was Will's deepest desire to see Africa one day. He talked about jungles and jungle critters incessantly. One day there was a dark skinned man driving a covered wagon who stopped at the Church. He enjoyed speaking with Will and told him he would give him a very rare creature if he would promise to take care of it.

Will was beside himself begging his Mother and Reverend Ben for permission to take on this challenge. The man, known as Charles, tried to prepare Will that this "pet" wasn't for everyone; that it took a very unusual family to accept this into their home. He said the pet required special care but also that the owners had to be careful to protect themselves as well. Will was overwhelmed with both childish and scientific curiosity. The Reverend said to Emily "as we sow so shall we reap" meaning they had raised an inquisitive son now they must accept how he was turning out.

And so Charles produced a huge glass jar, in and of itself a rarity in those times, with a wire cover. Inside that jar was what appeared to be a spider the size of a large bull frog. Will was enchanted and just a little horrified. His Mother was just plain horrified and the Reverend asked what its special needs and considerations were.

Charles said that they might have to arrange for a larger carrier for it if it seemed to grow. That it loved shade and cool damp places and that it liked meat, fresh raw meat, like scraps from a cut up chicken but that it didn't need to feed every day. Emily exclaimed "Grow?" to which Charles responded that he'd only seen a few of these and wasn't quite sure if this might not be a young one.

There was no giving it back. Will was too excited for words. He knew right where to keep it safe and happy in the basement of his home, a cool damp place. But, Charles continued, that he thought this spider, actually an arachnid and Will should look that up, could be dangerous to small animals. He went on to warn them that since it was not indigenous to that area he couldn't predict how it would react outside of its container. He urged them all to be certain it was properly housed.

No sooner had Charles left than Will started developing plans for his own museum of natural science. He had read about them but they were all in large cities or foreign places. He would have the only one in East Apple, Connecticut. They had taken a few trips to the nearest ocean beaches and he had already collected horseshoe crabs, star fish and mussel shells with Reverend Ben. And from the woods they had put together the skeletons of several birds, a rabbit and a deer. He would start gathering pine cones, empty birds' nests and nuts. Maybe his mother would help him draw some flowers he thought out loud. And so his boundless joy overcame their better judgment and the project which was to end so tragically was launched.

11

THE UNANSWERED PRAYER

I skipped ahead to the end of the manuscript because so much detail of their happy family was given that I felt I was prying simply reading the record she had left. It appeared almost blissful perhaps in part because Emily seemed grateful for every moment of this life. The Rev. Wilbur knew he was leading two lives with two wives living nearly next door to each other and no one was confronting him about this arrangement so he too was presumably grateful. He also was so proud of his son that at times he nearly told the truth from the pulpit. He had arranged with Emily, should the day come that he had passed on to the Lord and she was on her deathbed, she was to tell Will who his biological father was. She replied that she would be honored to do so but predicted that the Reverend would lead a long healthy life and one day himself tell the story to Will. Sadly, neither should have spent time with this concern.

Emily wrote: *Soon after Charles had gifted Will with the "spider" we discovered that it was not a juvenile but a female adult and she began laying eggs. Now aware of her gender Will named her Annabella. Will diligently prepared another cage for babies and soon he housed a small colony some of which we did release into the outer environs as we knew these creatures wouldn't survive in the New England climate; we simply could not keep them all.*

I am writing this on October 1, 1823. The dates given reflect when the incidents occurred but for the period of one year I have been unable to write; the reason for this you will soon understand by reading below. First I shall state that as a mother I was negligent in discerning the lengths Will would go to in attempting to keep those babies with Annabella. He established several secret sanctuaries for them within the cavernous cellar of our home.

September 30, 1822 Notes on Will

Following his recent 12th birthday Will began to receive correspondence in the mail regarding his "Museum". For his birthday he had asked to have flyers developed describing his Natural Science Museum. By this time he had a large collection of many interesting things and thought it was time to announce this to the world! He had drawn his own Monarch butterfly in one corner and a sketch of the Goliath arachnid was on the back where the addresses were to be placed. It was a real attention getter and he was most proud of it. We dutifully took it to the printer and had 50 copies made that he then addressed to "other museums" and universities within our nation. His father and I had to be firm when he wanted postage for the Louvre. Still we admired his sense of purpose and determination.

A few of the respondents appeared genuinely interested. They asked if there were any further sketches available and one university biologist inquired about the possibility of receiving a Goliath on loan or purchasing one of the offspring. Will grew quite excited by this request as we were always indicating that most of his ideas cost money to produce and he saw this as a way to invest back into his business. For example, he and his father could build storage cabinets for his specimens but he wanted glass for displaying many of these artifacts plus all materials cost something. And now he saw himself as needing a correspondence budget. How dear.

Well we made a date to receive the biologist and to house him for one night as he was taking on a three hour ride to get here. His arrival was a time of great pride for us all. Looking back I wish that day had never come. When we opened the cage to let the mother spider be examined she leapt out and disappeared into large cracks around the foundation. The scientist who had been about to express how impressed he was with the arachnid now ran in horror up the cellar stairs for the comfort of the kitchen. I too began to run and Will, who loved the spider dearly, just said "don't worry mother I shall retrieve Annabella!" Of course I didn't know she would be seeking to visit her kin.

The biologist, who had never unpacked, made haste to grab his satchel and was out the door and gone in an instant. Ben had planned to be home from Church duties for dinner with us all and would never have the opportunity to meet him. I caught my breath and then called down the stairs to Will: "How are you doing?" His response was "Almost got her back in the cage."

I went and got a glass of water from the pump to calm my nerves then called down again: "Do you need any help?" No response. I called a bit louder trying to keep fear out of my voice; still no reply. So I rushed down the stairs being careful to avoid Annabella should she happen to jump out at me. What I found was the most horrifying of sights, the most hideous a mother could ever conceive of and one which, try as I do, will never leave my memory.

Will was laying flat on the floor and Annabella and her offspring were feasting on his body – they were all over him! I have never screamed like this before but from the very base of my gut I let out a cry that I swear gave notice to Ben three miles away. Then I grabbed a broom in the corner of the cellar and started swatting at those disgusting arachnids with all my might: chasing them into corners and pounding on any that were within my reach. I kept on until only my boy remained in front of me. He had a pulse and the Lord must have given me a hand for I was able to get Will as far as the staircase when I miraculously heard the sound of Ben entering the house. I called to him and together we got Will up the stairs and onto a coach.

Both Ben and I were shaking and in tears as I explained what had occurred. Ben swallowed hard, said a brief prayer and said he would get our neighbor to fetch the doctor. Then we held our boy's hands, put hot cloths on his wounds thinking to draw the poison out, and prayed with great intensity but to no avail. By the time the doctor arrived we had lost the most golden child, the sweetest most intelligent young man I know the world would have seen. Our son was gone and we were inconsolable.

Part of the dilemma was that I could not give him up. I did not want Ben to take him to the Church but insisted he be laid out here, in his own home, with me to look after him. Ben was in nearly the same state I was and also had trouble suggesting a plan to which I might agree. He said certainly Will would stay with me for now. He would go inform the Church, his wife and girls and get some help in taking care of what needed to be done. He also said as an aside he would send one of the farmers over to see what he knew about eradicating any pests that might remain. I was so embittered at this point I said it was fine with me if we burned the farmhouse down and I would live in the barn. He held me a moment and said, "We shall work on this together. Just be patient you won't be alone for long".

Soon the church ladies came in carrying flowers and sweet soaps. We washed Will's desecrated bitten body and dressed him in his Sunday best then carefully transferred him to a bright red blanket and lay him on the buffet table. I cannot begin to describe what those wounds looked like. Not only must the detested beasts have bitten and poisoned him to render him helpless thus not permitting him to move, but they then bit into his flesh leaving deep gouges where hunks of meat, Will's dear body, had been sucked up into their mouths. I had to sit down quickly and was given smelling salts.

When Ben joined us it was obvious that he had been crying. All the ladies went to him and squeezed his arm or hugged him offering their condolences. They too were shedding tears. Will had been much loved. Ben brought condolences from many people including his wife and girls and then thanked the ladies for their time. He placed a bible in Will's stiff arms and, in front of the others, told me he would stay for a while and pray with me for Will's soul.

After they left we again had the discussion of where to bury Will. I insisted he should stay on my property; Ben argued the Church Cemetery up the hill and around the corner was the most appropriate place but I could not agree. We decided the next day was soon enough to let the workers begin to prepare the gravesite; the question would keep. Ben said he really wanted to stay with me that night but was fearful of his wife's reaction. I told him to please go along I was just going to sleep and I wasn't alone indicating Will. He kissed my forehead and said he would be back first thing in the morning.

Two things happened the next morning. Before Ben returned a neighbor with a large and prosperous farm came by. He must have left his place by 4:30 AM to have arrived so early. Ben had spoken to him the day before asking him to come and examine the arachnid situation and to make certain I would have no further problems with these monsters.

He was a nice fellow and very sorry for my loss. He then went down the stairs armed with a heavy shovel. He came back up about an hour later and stated that there was no longer any indication that these spiders existed; even their bodies were gone. He said many insects behaved the way ants do; who remove the bodies of their fallen comrades and return them to the nest. He went on to say that the colony had received a serious blow with the loss of their Mother and the deaths of so many workers. He had read that after suffering a serious defeat they had been known to crawl deep within the earth and to remain dormant for up to 100 years, perhaps longer. He was certain I should pay them no more worry.

I was relieved and chose to believe him as everything else so overwhelmed me. When Ben arrived the farmer again explained his analysis and left for home. I told Ben we should dig a deep hole in the cellar to be certain they were not living close to the surface. He agreed to send the gravediggers here first adding but then they must go up the hill. I acquiesced but metaphorically had my fingers crossed. There was no way that Will's body would leave my property.

After the wake the carpenter who built the pine caskets left two child-sized for us. The following morning a processional was to form at my house and walk with the coffin on a wagon taking my Will up the hill. Reverend Wilbur would perform a graveside ceremony as the weather was good of late, and Will so loved nature. But after the wake, when everyone was gone, Ben assisted me in placing Will in the other casket in the cellar and covering him over. We prayed, we sang and we wept then went upstairs to stuff the coffin for Will's approximate weight. An engraver had already been commissioned to prepare the stone. I insisted on the poem for it told the world that the boy was not truly lost to us but would reawaken with his arachnid family. One just had to know how to read it.

Shed not for him a single tear
Spare not for him your regret
'Tis but the body that lies here
The soul that graced it
Wanders yet!

And so I believe that Will has passed into the bodies of his arachnid
friends and is but lying dormant with them for however long it takes to
recover, stabilize and reenter the world. I saw where those that survived
my pounding with the broom scurried off to and know they are close-by.
Their bodies contain my Will.

After the mock burial at the cemetery on top of the hill, a place was
left in the graveyard for the stone which was being engraved. That would
signify Will's coffin although he is not in it. Rather he is home, where he
belongs, with me. When the graveside service ended I spoke privately to
Ben thanking him for the glorious time the three of us had shared but
releasing him now to spend his hours as needed by his family. He said he
would not be abandoning me. I took this to be a kindness but expected
him to go a separate way from me from this day forward.

When I returned to my now empty house I poured myself a glass of
sherry and went down to the cellar. Here I overturned an old crate and
sat upon it. I sipped the sherry and opened one of the books Will kept
in his museum area. It was titled World Map of Crustaceans, another
interest of Will's, and I began reading aloud. After a few minutes I heard
something behind me and saw that Ben was there. He said "It is much
too soon for you to be alone."

I replied that I did not feel alone and was enjoying reading to Will.
He said "Emily, my dearest, this is not going to be good for you. Let us
go upstairs for a little while and talk of what lies ahead."

85

We went upstairs and he reaffirmed his commitment to me! That we had a bond like no other and he would be back in the morning to drive me in to the Church where I was needed. I agreed to do as he wanted and so I left my home and Will for the better part of the next day.

12

THE PASTOR'S NEWS

I finally had to put the diary down but it was hard to stop reading. My heart had broken when Will died but of course he was born in 1811 so there was no way he, or any of them could still be living. I just had to think of it as a piece of history. Still I had a strong desire to find out two things as soon as possible: 1) How had things ended between the Reverend and Miss Harrison and 2) At what address had Miss Harrison lived; could this be her former home? Did this then account for my arachnids and was this why Wilbur's gravestone was in this yard? But before my mind could wander too far down this path Fred was knocking on the door and saying he brought the insulation men over to plan their work.

The insulation foreman discussed a couple of issues and gave me an estimate for blowing insulation into the walls rather than the clapboards having to be removed and large sheets of insulation inserted and then again covered over. I wanted to know what the blown-in insulation was made of and had it been treated with any chemicals. Once I was satisfied with his response I requested a written estimate and said we'd give him our answer by noon the next day. I wanted to make sure we would come in on target with our budget.

While Fred was still speaking with this foreman, so that there would be no gaps in the wall where the insulation could blow-out just as fast as they were pumping it in, I called Pastor Martin wondering if any church records would have the address of Miss Harrison's home. He said they had such records and asked me to hold while he searched for this as the church had recently computerized much information. Within moments he explained that houses in our town had not had numbers back then as the community was so small and everyone called for their mail at the Post Office; but he could tell me that she lived on Rattlesnake Hill Road. Interesting, I said, feeling greatly relieved, where is Rattlesnake Hill Road, I'd like to drive by her old place if it is still standing?

"Oh", he chuckled, "it's still standing and you are actually living in it!"

"What" was all I could manage to utter?

"Well", Pastor Martin continued, "Cemetery Hill Road was first called Rattlesnake Hill Road and for good reason. There were all manner of rattlers throughout those hills and rocks. But when it came time for maps to be made the consensus was that "Rattlesnake" was not a very positive descriptor, all residents could agree on that. Plus by that time there hadn't been a rattlesnake sighting in a decade, so they changed the name to reflect that it led to a significant cemetery which was important to the community history. There's a picture of the place right here and although it lacks some of your ells it is definitely the same structure."

"So this was the Harrison House?"

"Yes and the house had been built for Judge Rider" replied the Pastor. "The Judge had some problems due to the harshness of his punishments resulting in a few deaths so after he had stirred up considerable trouble he and his family moved away quickly selling everything to Miss Harrison's folks. She had been born to them later in life and they had already left a large farm to her brothers; now they got the Judge to say Miss Harrison could inherit their place, err, your place. They knew they hadn't much time left and wanted her to be secured in the community. And they were both dead within three years but she seemed able to deal with her independence."

"While you mention Judge Rider I must admit I am curious about what actually got him to leave the house. You know Priscilla Austin up the hill from me? Well she started to tell me the story but then seemed to think better of it and changed the subject."

"I suppose there's no harm in telling you what I've heard" said Pastor Martin seeming a bit reticent, "As they are all long departed now at any rate. Tell me how much have you heard?"

I mentioned that the widow, who had also lost her son to suicide in this, the Judge's home, then began erecting hangman's scaffolding in the yard to frighten the Judge's family and the Judge turned her over to the authorities.

The Pastor began: "Apparently the widow was so angry at the Judge's lack of a heart and felt so justified believing he had caused her son's suicide that she didn't try to conceal her sinister intentions. She reportedly told the Constable 'An Eye for an Eye'. After the Constable and the Judge conferred it was determined that this widow would have to appear before the Judge in his chamber, the home where her son had perished!

"Everyone was shocked. How could this possibly be resolved? What would be her next move? Well it didn't take long to find out.

"The next day her nearest neighbors reported to the Constable that the widow had sent her children to them with a note saying 'please look after the girls for a day or so'. After hearing this, the constable stopped by the widow's farm but the only one around was another neighbor who had showed up to cut wood. It was his turn to help, you see. This man had no idea where the widow was.

"The next morning revealed the horror I'm not sure you will care to hear. It can only be believed if you can imagine the depth of her grief leading her to insanity. For certainly she was no longer in her right mind to have done this as her anger at the Judge truly made her wish to take the life of his son. But this murderous desire was thwarted by the Judge keeping his son and wife inside their home and literally hiring men to guard them while the widow was free. Probably the Judge supposed she would soon be jailed although this was most uncommon for a woman.

"In any case her solution was grim. She had spent the time while her daughters were gone working way out back at her farm digging in the small family graveyard. She exhumed her boy's body, which having been in the earth for nearly two months with no box around it, was quite disintegrated and wormy. They said it was more of a moldy skeleton. Apparently she wrapped it into a tarp and during dark of night dragged it the 3 miles to the Judge's home. This did the corpse no further good as you can well imagine.

"When his Mrs. Rider entered the kitchen to start the morning fire she glanced out to find the scaffolding resurrected and human remains hanging from it. There was also a sign on it reading 'You done this.'

"The poor wife screamed bringing her household running and the Judge was soon out the door with his shot gun and a bull whip. Apparently the night guard now ran forward and had to own up to the fact that he might have fallen asleep briefly during the wee hours of the morning. He was lucky the Judge did not shoot him. Rather this man was assigned the hideous task of bringing down both body and scaffolding and told to burn the latter. Then he was to go and fetch the Constable while the Judge made certain the widow wasn't lurking about the property.

"But she was. She came at the Judge from the back as he was inspecting his barn. She had an axe and he did not hesitate to step back from her and using the whip, removed the weapon from her hand. She was hysterical and was quickly subdued but it took the Judge's entire family to accomplish this.

"While they were tying her at wrists and ankles for the safety of all, she was spewing venomous curses. The most potent of these was that a son born of this house could not flourish but would perish by the age of 12. She knew the Judge's son was but 10 years old and she was cursing him, and the family through him. She was still screaming these curses as they took her to jail; at that time there was no local place for the mentally ill.

"It was directly after this that the Judge and family decided to join the wife's family in Massachusetts. They soon sold their place to the Harrisons and facilitated it being inherited by Miss Emily in the future. In fact, because she was known to be a spinster and likely to stay as such, it seemed a safe move to make given the curse and all."

I thanked Pastor Martin and returned to my chores with Fred and the other contractors but felt gobsmacked by this news.

13

OVERWHELMED

Instead of hunting for answers to questions which were plaguing me I now felt overwhelmed with answers that were impossible to comprehend. The biggest one which caused me the most horror was where was Wilbur's body buried? This appeared to be answered but I feared the answer would drive me mad. According to Emily's diary he was not in any cemetery, he was not even interred in the backyard; his remains were lying in the dirt in the very cellar of our home! He was resting just a few feet below me. And he did not have the good graces to repose by himself but the cellar was literally the colony of his arachnid population whether they 'be living or they be dead'.

Add his mother's poem to this scenario, especially the phrase "the soul who graced it wanders yet" and it is little wonder that I have nightmares. At these realizations I now set the diary down where I was reading in the front parlor and bolted up the stairs to our bedroom. I began furiously searching the bottom drawer of a dresser where I had simply stuffed many items with which I could not bear to part but which were most unlikely to be of future use to me. Here I finally found a small box of jewelry from my teenage years in Roma. Carefully wedged into one corner and wrapped in a small plastic bag was a cross I had purchased in the Vatican City; it was in the gift shop attached to St. Peter's.

This was most certainly a time I would need help from the Holy Father on up! My cross was made of tiny ceramic stones set in gold and on a gold chain. You would not precisely identify it as a crucifix but part of its artistic value was the assumption of Christ on a cross as indicated by flesh toned stones on the center with strategically located red dots at hands, side and feet; there was also a brown circle surrounding the area appearing to be His head. This, of course, was the crown of thorns. In any case due to its Holy origin at the Vatican I now placed this necklace around my own neck and instantly felt a sense of both peace and strength.

Thus adorned I made my way down two flights of stairs to the cellar. I approached the probable gravesite and said "Hello Will, I've been anxious to meet you but probably not here. Have you any plans to rise up and greet us?" Then I held my breath using all my strength to keep from running to the stairs. There was no reply, not even a tremor of the ground or the movement of a mouse or spider. "Well," I announced, "let's keep it this way until we can think of where to move you." And I hastily returned to the first floor before he could change his mind.

I sat down rather heavily mulling over all I had read and done today. I wondered if we needed permission to exhume a body. I would think not as it was located in an illegal grave, on the other hand he was no kin to me and might have the right to eternal rest depending upon one's view of these matters. When Matt returned I would have to get his opinion on this. I knew one cannot go into the burial grounds of ancient peoples and simply disrupt their graves by

CYNTHIA HERBERT BRUSCHI ADAMS

building new homes or shopping malls on top of them. Those sites must be honored and treated with dignity. In many cases I believe the builders' plans are thwarted.

The next most horrifying information I had learned from Emily's diary was the confirmation that what we had found in the cellar were, in fact, Goliath Bird Eating spiders just as Peter had said! Had my disgusting arachnids come from a traveling medicine show which brought exotic spiders from the Amazon to live in Emily and Will's home? That an adult man had knowingly provided these abominations to a young boy with only a proviso to be careful? And worst of all there was the fact these spiders had lived in the house since something like 1820?

They could be anywhere and everywhere. We had fumigated the cellar, and it sounds like the cellar was a climate which they enjoyed, but at this point they could reside in the walls, the ground, the barn floors, and even the attic if they found the right space! They could have moved to the neighbors or migrated to the sheds which had existed where I found the shards of bones! If they were still here and alive after 200 years then they were totally acclimated and could be living just about anywhere they wanted to!

At this point I was unable to stand my own clothing; I felt like I was crawling with bugs. These worries made me perspire and it had been a long day. I went into our little ground floor laundry room to strip down before again going upstairs. Why bring dirt through the house I reasoned. Once upstairs I laid out a comfortable loose fitting sundress, a pair of fresh sandals and entered the shower. I was completely immersed in warm water and soap while shampooing my long hair which became a lighter shade of brown as it got cleaner. My mind wandered and I thought, "How interesting that my eyes are brown like my mother's but my skin and hair coloring are more like my dad's." Then the thought "Shoot, it must be way past time to feed the kitten," and then I felt her furry little body rub against my leg. What crossed my mind now was that "She must really be hungry to come into the shower!" But when I peeked out through the soap and bubbles all I saw was horror.

A kitten had not scurried under the shower curtain but one of the smaller Goliath Bird Eaters had. There was an arachnid, nearly as large as Sybil, clinging to my ankle. The water continued streaming down but the creature behaved as though oblivious. I didn't know whether to shake my leg, swat at the beast or to simply start running through the house. With little self control I chose the latter hoping to get the spider to voluntarily remove itself without risking angering it. I had reverted to flight behavior rather than choosing to fight it.

I dashed through the upstairs without stopping to turn off the shower. The old shower curtain that had been functioning there for years was ripped from its rod in the process. Water was gushing out behind me as I ran for my life. I slipped a little on the wet floor but as I jerked to save myself from a fall the hairy disgusting beast clung onto my leg. Screaming and crying out for help I continued my frantic path through the house nearly flying down the upstairs staircase and thus having to grab onto the railing to avoid going head first into the wall below. But my erratic, jerky motions did not dislodge my companion. I ran even faster once on the ground floor and continued my rant at the hideous spider hoping that my loudness might send it away, but to no avail. I instinctively headed for the kitchen which was always my safe haven. I knew we had roach poison under the sink and my plan was to unleash the contents of that can onto my ankle whether or not it burned my skin.

As I neared the sink a sense of relief beset me; I would soon be free of this loathsome burden. And then, just as surprising as had been its entry into the shower, it was gone. I stared around me as I started shivering in the kitchen. It was not that I was cold but shock had set in. Still my practical side took over. I hesitantly climbed back upstairs always at the ready to fight this creeping crawling gargoyle for I now held the poison spray. I saw nothing, not a sign of it, not a motion out of place, not a wet streak, nothing. I reentered the bathroom and shut off the shower attempting to prevent the ceiling from collapsing onto the downstairs. Luckily much of the water had gone down the drain once my body stopped deflecting it toward the room. I pulled out all of our towels and laid them on the wet floor. Then, almost seeming to sleep walk, I went back downstairs and waited for help.

When Matt got home thirty minutes later I was still sobbing in the living room and basically incoherent. He tried to empathize but he could not understand what I was saying or imagine why I was naked although initially he had hoped that was a pleasant surprise. I continued to stammer that "it came up the plumbing" but I could not articulate what had arrived in this manner. Matt accurately guessed the upstairs shower was the plumbing in question and when I finally said "arachnid" he seemed to understand.

He said "Elena Maria please calm down and have a little wine" which he offered. Matt then inspected the entire house because I was not certain at what point the arachnid had jumped off my body. Thankfully I had not been bitten but in one way this did not help as Matt was left wondering if my drama was actually based on reality. He finished making dinner while I dressed and we agreed the plumbers could investigate further the next day.

When we went to bed that evening I placed a mat and several bricks over the opening of the shower drain and laid a crucifix on top of the bricks. I thought I would contact the plumbers and the exterminators, if Peter was up and running again or would consider returning after his ordeal in our basement; and I also decided that my next shower would be downstairs. However my uneasy feeling would not go away as I still did not know where today's spider had jumped off or where it might now be hiding.

When morning arrived I found my priorities had changed. I wanted to know more about what to expect from these creatures. Maybe they considered the moist, dark, warm insides of our drains as their habitat; after all, the house had lain vacant for years. Perhaps they were curious about where the warm water was coming from since we moved in or had they recently moved into the pipes when we fumigated their cellar air? As I thought these things I crossed myself and wished there was a Catholic church in East Apple. I needed a priest and a vial of Holy Water!

I was sure there was an entomologist at the University, maybe a whole department, time to look them up. Going to the internet I discovered there was a department and it was far ranging; the world is full of bugs, and there was a professor named April Yantz who specialized in The Amazon. I hastily hit her highlighted phone number. When she answered I could not talk fast enough to be sure she understood what these critters were and my urgent need to control them before they took over our house. I even name dropped that my husband was in the psychology department and that we were newly settling into the community. If this engendered her sympathy I would gratefully accept it.

Dr. Yantz said she was teaching class in about thirty minutes and had a pretty full day but could swing by on her way home around five thirty if that worked for us. She wanted to get a look at the spiders for herself or at least a sense of where they might be living. She hung up by saying "be careful." Great advice I thought and so I spent an anxious day trying to stay away from our cellar and to have upbeat thoughts about the house.

She arrived well before Matt made it home. She wasn't what I expected but then how many entomologists had I met? She was short but very athletic looking as though she hiked through woods and fields lifting rocks and digging into trees to conduct her research. She wore no makeup looking as though she would simply roll out of the tent on a safari morning and immediately start seeking jungle bugs. She was enthusiastic regarding this project and seemed to cringe a bit when I described our recent extermination adventures. "Well", she added, "let's start exploring, I can usually tell immediately if Goliaths have been around but you know it is perfectly normal for them to disappear for extended periods of dormancy if the nest has been endangered, and then reappear when they want to breed again or feel the environment is now safe. So even if we don't find them you shouldn't be disappointed they may still very well be around."

"Disappointed isn't exactly how I would characterize my emotions," I explained. "We just need to know what we are up against and what is the best way to handle them for the good of all?" I didn't want her to think I was not a friend of ecology and evolution but the biological reality of sharing our home with these large and dangerous arachnids was nothing I had bargained for when we assumed ownership of this home. And although we hired a thorough inspection of the premises it is probably not typical for a home inspector to dig into the ground looking for dormant giant spiders.

April began at the top, as she described it, by going to the attic and examining floor dust and the cracks and crevices along the sides of the attic where the floor ran up against the roof. She even examined the rafters and edges of the chimney coming up through the house completing her efforts by hunting through an old nail keg residing there as well as any older looking rolls of wallpaper or ancient boxes. After declaring this area "Goliath free" she walked slowly down the attic staircase with a flashlight in one hand and a long nail-like implement in the other. I presumed this nail looking instrument must have been to scrape any spot that might be clotted up with dirt but it could also serve as a spike to put through the heart of a giant arachnid. I liked the idea that she carried a defense weapon.

She repeated all this inspecting again throughout the second floor which was where I had my encounter the day before. Here she paid particular attention to the shower drain and the sink drain too. With her light shining into the drain I thought she flinched slightly as though she had seen something move but when I queried her she denied seeing anything. "Just being careful" she observed. She was also meticulous when inspecting the fireplaces especially around the mantels. To my question here she replied that the fireplaces were a direct connection to the cellar as well as to each other room that had a fireplace making them a logical conduit. She also noted that if the day came when we added air conditioning those ducts would make a handy pathway for the spiders when the air wasn't turned on. This was not a comforting thought but I made a mental note to stuff all openings if such a luxury as air conditioning was ever added.

The first floor required much more time due to its proximity to the cellar, being connected via one staircase; its many doorways leading to the outside plus two sets of stairs leading up. Matt arrived before this floor was completed. I could tell he was hungry and perhaps a little disconcerted to have a stranger going through his home. While he settled in, April and I went down in the cellar and began another detailed inspection. Here she commented that she was seeing a few tracks and a little of the goo they typically ooze to begin nest making but she could not yet determine how recent these signs were.

With that pronouncement, and a glance out back noting we have several outbuildings, she asked if she might resume inspecting tomorrow. I quickly agreed. Although I had been anxious to know where these beasts were actually living, the length of time this was taking was beginning to wear me out. I reasoned if they have been here for 200 years I could probably wait another day to find them out.

Matt and I enjoyed a quiet evening followed by a first floor shower and then early to bed. I wish I could report a good night's rest but as soon as the bedroom was dark my imagination brightened. I had to be certain that Matt's hairy leg resting next to my leg was just that, Matt's leg, not some creature. Once the clouds passed over the moon I started seeing odd shadows moving on the walls but after getting up twice to touch those spots I was reassured that they were simply reflections from objects in the room. Our windows were open a bit for airflow which also permitted night sounds to enter our chamber. I intensely concentrated on these various sounds in order to reassure myself we were not about to encounter a sneak attack by a herd of Goliaths. Fearful as I was, the crickets remained crickets and only an occasional automobile passed by on the road. At 1 AM I was exhausted and finally fell asleep.

That was when the dreams started. I don't remember many details but at one point Emily was in our bedroom wearing white and saying she had to show me something, please come and follow her. She placed her finger across her lips indicating I must be quiet to avoid waking Matt. Then she faded out and the woman I had pictured as the tormentor of Judge Rider appeared. She wanted me to come outside and give her my opinion of the new gallows she had built. Finally she disappeared and April was standing by the bed holding a skewer of Goliath arachnids and wondering if I would like to join her outside for a barbeque.

The dreams finally ended when I apparently screamed "NO, JESUS, NO!" And I awoke in bed clinging to Matt who simply rolled over and patted my shoulder. A little later he had to shake me a bit to get me to awaken. I told him I'd had terrible nightmares and he said he was sorry to hear that. Then as he gazed out our side window he asked if I knew why there were scorch marks in the grass next to the shed?

14

PROPERTY CONCERNS

B efore I could think of other more mundane things like completing construction plans and grocery shopping I had to know about some of the deed questions that arose as I read parts of Emily's diary concerning Mrs. Bridgefield. Shortly prior to our closing on this property the Town of East Apple and our Bank required that we have a title search conducted. Matt and I agreed that was a great requirement for we certainly didn't wish to begin work on a property, including expensive materials and upgrades, and then have someone waltz in and say we were actually squatting on their home. What a waste of our time and money that would be so our Attorney, Larry Dougal, who was to do our Closing had his office produce a Title Search, naturally ahead of that step.

As I understand it a Title Search involves looking back at all prior property owners and any registered deeds or liens on the property just to be certain everything is either paid off or properly closed from one owner to the next. For example if the current owner had not paid their property taxes we might be forced to cover that cost before we could assume ownership: an expense most would not wish to incur on top of a new mortgage. And with a house of this age it could be anticipated that there were numerous owners. In fact there were several some rather curious, and there had been subdivisions.

The original farm, which the Judge had first owned, followed by Emily's parents, then Emily encompassed a significant tract of land. The original deed did not speak in terms of acreage but described the boundaries as "beginning where Snake Hill Road intersected with Butterfly Meadow Road heading north and covering both sides of Snake Hill until the rise where there is a stand of pines near a stonewall." Of course everyone in that time knew of these markers but as folks passed on and left divisions of the land to more than one child, or sold off a portion and gave meadows away, or even paid taxes by turning some land over to the Town, you can see it became increasingly difficult to demonstrate what you owned. Also a stand of pines can be cut down or destroyed by fire and road names are subject to changes thus these descriptions have many limitations.

So when a measurement of "acres" became the mode of measurement it was thought to denote a vast improvement. However, there really weren't surveyors available with fine instruments to delineate the number of acres a parcel held. More likely the farmer/owner walked the land with his bordering neighbor and they agreed to boundaries if that part of land were not intersected by roadways. If stonewalls existed they were typically agreed to be markers and many times these walls were co-owned by siblings inheriting land to be divided. The reality of this was that "acres" were then an estimate often with wide variations. Some folks accepted that they owned '40 acres' as a deed stated but the equal half of this divided property might contain a much larger tract of '40 acres' based purely on old estimates. Not an exact science by any means and thus the need for

Judges, constables and mediators at the banks if "understandings" fell apart.

I even read one story of a man and his two oldest sons trying to move a stone wall around a walnut tree so that they could acquire the nuts. They worked on nights when the moon was large and there were no clouds but by daylight the wall appeared so jagged that they were found out, chastised by the Town and had to put the wall back to its original configuration. The brother that they had endeavored to fleece had his wife make them a walnut pie but instead of using molasses and maple sugar to sweeten it she prepared it with molasses, maple sugar and just enough cod liver oil to cause those who ingested it to spend the night in their outhouse; yet that fishy flavor escaped detection. Such was justice in that era.

It is easy to see then why we were quite happy to comply with this Title Search regulation. I was fascinated to review the report that was produced by Larry's office. For whatever reason the Wilbur name had not stuck to my brain at the time of the closing, but he must have appeared as an add-on to his wife, Emily Harrison – if in fact they married. However I am certain I recall the name of Edwin Thompson who now turns out to be the brother of Mrs. Bridgefield. He was listed as receiving a subdivision of the land not too long after Emily Harrison left her inheritance. I wonder how this came to pass. There is also a column on these sheets that indicates the price paid for various parcels of land. On Edwin's lot it seems to indicate the land was a gift from Theodor Mills. Who Theodor Mills was and how he fits into all this still remains to be seen but my curiosity was peaked.

As I review these things there is also a more personal question in the back of my mind. I'm wondering how I'm really doing with Matt. Maybe I can use these findings to get a sense of how he is feeling towards people in general and me in particular. Although we continue to make love recent events have cut down on frequency and I miss it.

15

INTO THE WOODS

Matt's study on Multiple Personality disorders raised a question for me regarding what was going on with his mind. I had never seen him behave towards anyone the way he had toward the graduate student who messed up when explaining too much about their research to a participant. Was his investigation led by his own personal need to understand this mental condition better? Had I married a sweet man who had a complete and distinct alter ego about whom he was not even fully aware? One who operated to control, punish and humiliate others? Or was something else going on?

Ever since the night I had walked in on Matt belittling his graduate student I wondered if many of the ways he denied my fears or corrected what I thought as though not serious, was actually gaslighting. If Matt was mercurial anything was possible. Gaslight was a 1944 movie about a woman being manipulated by her husband into thinking she was insane. He wanted to gain control of her and get rid of her. He undermined her confidence until she didn't know what to believe because, of course, she trusted her husband. Well, Matt didn't seem to think it was significant that someone shut Peter the exterminator into the cellar and blocked the door but I was convinced that whoever this person was they were guilty of attempted murder.

Many times Matt said I was making too much of something or taking it too seriously. While we can all be overly sensitive, if we are frequently told that our reactions are not appropriate, it doesn't take long for self-doubt to kick in and wear away at our self-esteem. Was my husband consciously doing this? And if so why? Also the number of traumas and surprises I had recently suffered caused me to fall back on some of my more superstitious beliefs. Did he take this for cracks in my sanity?

Yet another consideration was the pressure he was under to complete enough significant studies, get them published and reviewed, so that he would be granted tenure. And we had just moved so nothing was settled at home. Would he again be the man I thought I married once tenure was awarded? If I could only get more answers to some of the mysteries that still haunted me then I could relax. It seemed to me that the people next door and probably Adam and Priscilla had information I needed.

Maybe it was time to get a little help; help that I could trust one hundred per cent without a doubt, I called my parents and asked if they could join us the following weekend. My mother answered the phone and was very pleased with the invitation. They still had not seen the property due to many things which had occurred in all of our lives and especially around our move. But, as I am an only child, they said yes and mother was immediately planning what she could bring to feed us. I was happy to agree to everything she suggested since our cooking space is still so poor and as she is a fantastic cook. I also knew Matt would be very busy but could at least have meals with us. This would give my mother more time to pick-up on anything off about him, IF there was anything.

I desperately wanted Matt to be the good guy I loved but so many strange things had gone on I just needed some assurances. If all he needed was to have more research time I would be the happiest wife a tenure track professor ever had!

Getting the house ready for overnight guests was both daunting and exciting: daunting because there were many tasks needing to be done just to make another bedroom habitable; exciting because there was a real pleasure in knowing my parents would be here together in our first home. I began by choosing the Judge's old chambers to serve as their bedroom. I didn't do this because of its jaded history but because it was a room as large as our master bedroom, it had three lovely windows and a fireplace complete with original mantel. The wallpaper was old, floral and stained, just begging to be taken down and redone, but I was certain my folks would see through that to the room's future beauty.

We had piled a few boxes in one corner of this room on top of what should serve as their dresser so I began unpacking what I could find places for and moving boxes to less central areas. It wasn't too long before I had found the pad, sheets, pillows and quilt which should help to make up their bed. I piled scatter rugs in one doorway; this room had both a front stair and a back stair exit, so that I could take them outside for shaking or beating. Before I returned the rugs to this floor I would also vacuum it and move the dresser closer to their bed. Somewhere I was sure to find a nightstand and place that and a floor lamp near the bed allowing for easy nighttime reading should they so desire.

The closet was more of a disaster. To begin with whoever the ancient wallpaper hanger had been had taken a short cut in decorating.

The wallpaper which covered the walls in this room did not continue in the closet. Opening the closet door gave one a sense of stepping even deeper into the past. It was clearly something from the 1920's. Amusing.

Our bedroom was the mirror image of this room, each room constructed on either side of the enormous chimney, with one exception: our closet was so shallow it barely accommodated the width of one hanger. We had but a few possessions in there and were temporarily using coat racks throughout the room. I hated the idea of cutting the room up to allow for a deeper closet but thus far we hadn't figured what else we might do if we wanted our clothing in the same room with us and not on a bed in a room down the hall. Lack of closet space is a frequent complaint of those with old houses. When this house was built most folks did not have large wardrobes and rooms were trimmed by pegged boards which held whatever needed hanging.

I finished preparing my folks' room and planned to cut fresh flowers to place in vases on their mantel and in the bathroom we would share upstairs; at least the plumbing had been repaired and the shower curtain was new. There was also to be an outside concert at the University this weekend which we would delight in attending. It would give my parents another glimpse into the agreeableness of this area.

By the time they arrived on Friday evening Fred and I had actually created more makeshift counter space in the kitchen and had cleared off an actual table in the dining room so that we could eat as a family. I placed our Civil War soldier's painting at an advantage to the table for a total historical mood. Even Sybil was acting like she knew something was about to happen as she rubbed around the table legs.

Our evening was joyous, warm and happy. My parents said many positive things about the potential they saw in this house. Matt came home early enough to help me prepare this first "official meal" as we assumed we'd enjoy Mother's food over the next few days. When we brought my folks and their suitcases upstairs my Mother hesitated at the door, it was only for a moment but it was almost as though something had caught her heel midair and would not release it for a moment. She quickly seemed herself again but did ask if we were aware of anything tragic ever happening in that room? I answered that it had been a Judge's chamber and there may have been "bad karma" in the room 200 years ago but we knew of nothing terribly tragic happening in this room. However, full disclosure, we did reveal that there was rumored to have been a suicide somewhere in the house during that same period. "Well", she added "the houses in Italy are so old there is always scandal and death on the doorsteps." That comment made me feel that our problems were just normal life.

When we entered our bedroom they both exclaimed at how well our collected antiques were fitting into the room including our canopy bed. They thought it was lovely until I laughed and showed them our closet's interior. "If a heavy set person ever wanted to hide in our closet they'd never survive" I noted. It was then that my dad looked around the hall and then began taping on the back of the closet door. After a moment he asked for a flashlight and appeared to step through the closet and into a room heretofore unknown to us. The back of the closet was a hidden door and behind it was a dusty little room with a trapdoor and folding stairs which descended into the cellar! "Wow" I said, "Isn't this cool." but had no idea why it had been kept hidden from us while we were buying the house.

My Dad's explanation for the secret panel was that at some point, probably early in the history of the house, an owner had needed a secret way to get in and out of the home. Once that person moved on or moved out no one may have noticed that there was unexplained space back there. It was really charming to have such a mystery, even so, hard to believe because as recently as sixty years ago or so workers had put plumbing into the room next door when they created a bathroom out of what had been a nursery: surprising that the carpenters or plumbers wouldn't have noticed the room at that time even if not the panel.

We all agreed that this just added to the character of the house and was part of why one enjoyed an older home. I imagined playing hide and seek up here one day with our future children and having them surprised when Mommy would go into one room and come back up from downstairs. What fun it could be. However a second and more practical thought was to work around the trap door but turn this space into the master bedrooms walk-in closet.

Matt said "Tomorrow, although I have to go into the University for a while, Elena Maria will show you the grounds and her interesting findings from digging near the walls." My dad asked "Old bottles and hardware?" To which Matt responded "And then some but I'll let her show you tomorrow." Then Matt gave me a wink and I smiled demurely indicating yes, somethings would have to wait until tomorrow.

When Matt left after my Mother's hearty breakfast I was rather excited to begin the tour of the barn and our thirty acres. I had only been way back on the property at the time we were deciding to make an offer on buying the place so this would be an adventure for me as well as something new to them. I felt certain we couldn't get lost because the chimney of our house rose so high on the horizon; at least that was what I had been told. Anyway it was a most secure feeling for me to have both my parents together with me at the same time. We filled a couple water jugs, took a little bread and cheese and prepared to head out for an exploration making certain to leave Sybil in the house.

Our property was oblong, shaped like a railroad car. There was sufficient frontage on the road but as the property had been cut up with subdivisions of the original farm, large hunks had been removed along the road thus leaving us with acreage that went straight back, behind the house. The other properties which were built along the road and were now the neighbors of our house also had their land behind them. This created a large forest where the overgrown fields from the original farm had long since returned to woods. It was a lovely feeling to be surrounded by trees and we enjoyed the many varieties of birds that were drawn to this area. Naturally other wild creatures moved here including deer, coyotes and fisher cats as well as the smaller woodland critters such as squirrels, chipmunks, rabbits, skunks and opossums. We knew we would require high fences around gardens and fruit trees if we hoped to protect them from the deer which seemed to present the greatest threat to our desired lifestyle; but deer and all of nature were a major part of this property's charm.

We started our nature walk going toward the eastern edge of our property where the ground still held a few traces of an old logging road. This featured ruts where only grass was growing. Around these ruts were ferns, brambles and an abundance of trees. The trees were multiple sizes and would necessitate some thinning to keep the woodland healthy. There were a few fir trees but mostly oak, ash, maple and a bit of poplar. The thickness of the woods added to its beauty and mystery for you could not see far out when the leaves were fully opened as they now were.

We hiked and stumbled a bit as we attempted to go directly north toward the back of our property. Just beyond what felt like the midway point my father stopped and pointed toward the west side of our land and up at tree level. My first thought was that he had spotted a turkey in a branch or perhaps an owl; we had already sent a family of five deer running, but instead we discovered he was pointing at a tarp hanging over a rope connected to two parallel trees. That was odd we all said rather at the same time. I offered it might belong to hunters who had written permission to use a neighbors' land and may have unknowingly over extended their territory. We switched our direction toward this tarp in order to investigate further.

What we saw made my jaw drop. There was a small clearing which had been hacked out leaving the ground bare in the center of which someone had rolled stones together forming a fire pit. The rocks bore charred sides toward their center and several clean sticks were leaning on a nearby tree. There was a crude hammock between other trees and a rather limp looking small tent not far from the fire. A few pots and pans were also clustered near the tent but one thing struck me with a shock as I continued my hasty inventory of the camp: my lawn chair was sitting between the tent and the fire with a dirty shirt strewn across its back. This was the home of our thief! He apparently kept a close watch on our house from our property for whatever he needed and very likely those pots and pans were the items Carol, Tamisha and Easton had reported missing as well.

"What should we do" I asked feeling especially grateful to be with my parents? My mother responded "Well let's take a few photos and then grab your lawn chair!" My father agreed but added "He may be watching us right now so just take the lawn chair and don't express any aggression toward the other items." Although that sounded like good advice I had to add "But he's on our property!" "Yes", said my Dad, but he may be someone who has trouble understanding distinctions like that." I wasn't quite sure I agreed but did as he said.

A little unnerved by this unexpected finding I suggested we turn back and try the walk again later. Once the mention had been made that we might be under observation, at that very moment, we all agreed to return to the house and have the picnic in our yard. Also, I had not secured the back door and our "overly friendly" neighbor might have known the house was empty. I didn't want to find anything else missing.

I texted Matt just to keep him in the loop but he did not respond. Most likely he was tied up with his students or perfecting the research and writing. I then called the local resident State Trooper to report someone illegally using our land and perhaps engaging in petty thievery. They apparently weren't particularly busy as a Trooper said he'd be right over.

When he arrived he looked at our cell pictures and asked that we send them to his phone as evidence. He then wanted a copy of our property map which, as a new home owner, I was easily able to provide. Finally he asked if someone would mind showing him where the camp was. My father was happy to oblige so they headed out into the woods. Mother and I went to our favorite comfort zone, the kitchen, where we began preparations for a robust, multi-course Italian dinner for the evening. She had brought two firm eggplants, a jar of her own sauce, hard Parmesan cheese for grating, good Chianti, special egg noodles, beef steak and mushrooms; she asked if this would be enough!

When the officer returned to the house with dad he said they caught a glimpse of the guy as they quietly approached the encampment. He looked fairly young and very scruffy as though he did not use running water and only owned the clothing on his back. I added to the story the information from the students next door and from our realtor Adam who appeared to know something he wouldn't say. I asked the students and Adam to join us as soon as possible mentioning we were entertaining a State Trooper as well as my folks.

Tamisha was the first to speak declaring that she figured someone had been trying to scare them away with all that phony moaning in the night. Adam decided to come clean about what he had heard. It seems the Macintoshes had three boys the youngest of whom was not mentally stable. His folks had trouble dealing with him but since he was an adult now the courts would not get involved until or unless he committed a crime. Finally his folks decided to sell their home and move away from him since he would not leave on his own.

Once the house was on the market his pranks exacerbated. He would watch customers come and go from some hiding place in the woods or perhaps on another level of their very house. When any family made a return visit he would cause the moaning, shut doors from the outside so that the prospects might become temporarily trapped in a room, and change the furniture arrangement from basically conservative to extremely bizarre during the same visit. He even would booby-trap something within the customers' car such as grease on a key hole or a flat tire. These actions were nothing particularly criminal but annoying and stressful, especially if repeated several times, or if the customer had any fears or misgivings of their own. It certainly appeared to be criminal mischief was my thought.

I asked Adam what had happened to this son. Adam said there were many complaints about him and in the end the Macintoshes claimed they had taken him with them to Kentucky. Adam added "He may have gone but from what I am hearing he's back now and up to his old behaviors."

"And what's driving him" my mother asked? Adam's reply was that "He didn't want anyone else living in his folks' house and wanted to get rid of anyone who tried to buy it." Adam then noted, of course the house had been sold. The Trooper said he'd be in touch with Social Services and see if they couldn't get him some help. This sounded like an excellent idea.

Three days passed and the Trooper called to inform us that Social Services had closed the case. The Macintoshes confirmed to them that Joseph, their son, had indeed been spending time in East Apple, CT but was now relocated with them in Kentucky. It had frightened him to know that Social Services wanted to "help" him so he had fled our State for Kentucky. The parents could not guarantee how long he would remain with them but they hoped he would at least be there through Christmas.

I thanked the Trooper.

16

THE REVEREND'S CONFESSION

The remainder of my parents' visit was less consequential: we found no more trap doors or hidden camps. We still weren't sure where the Macintoshes' son was living or camping but somehow knowing that there was an actual living entity making those eerie sounds helped to decrease my fear. Sybil was doing well and Matt had passed "the Mother test"; that is, she saw no strange behavior nor did his presence arouse concern in her that he was evil in any way or that he would do me harm. The workmen were coming pretty much as expected and Fred was always here either supervising or building or both.

I decided this was a good time to read more of Miss Emily's diary. When I left off she had been talking about returning to her duties at the Church as Rev. Wilbur's secretary and companion as it where. She made note that she believed Ben to be encouraging her to come back to work as he was worried about her mental state. She wrote:

By early October, 1822 I had managed to leave my home and poor Will for the day in order to be of help or at least encouragement to Ben. He had convinced me to do so right after the "interment" at the top of the hill. He wanted to talk about our loss and soon I was able to say what a smart son we had and how talented and good natured he was but I spoke mostly of Will in the present tense. This did not go unnoticed and Ben gently reminded me that our boy was now with his Heavenly Father. "Perhaps he is" I allowed at one point, "Or he may lie dormant with his pets waiting for the right time to emerge like Christ from the tomb."

Ben cut me off a bit harshly. "If others hear you speak thusly" he said, "You will be accused of blasphemy and they may not understand it is but your grief that makes you speak this way." He further entreated me to take care of what I said and to whom adding no one would rather see Will's smiling face than would he but he had to force himself to accept God's will no matter how painful. "God's Will," I thought, "What an interesting phrase under these circumstances."

Things went along like this for a few days. I would insist on staying by myself in my home at night but would return to the office first thing every morning and help with all Church matters just as before. One evening Ben made a surprise visit simply to see how well I was actually doing. By the time he arrived I had already set up my nighttime place in the cellar near to the spot in which we had laid Will to rest. As he had a key I never even heard him enter the house until he was on the cellar stairs and I was already caught. He ran his fingers through his hair and said "Dear Emily, you must not live this way! You will lose your mind and also become ill from this damp dark place. Please you must promise me to sleep in your own bed up stairs."

Rather sarcastically and totally out of character for me I retorted "And will you sneak out every night to be sure I am in the correct room?" Then I fell to weeping and so did he.

We went upstairs to the kitchen where I made us both chamomile tea from my herb garden and we talked at length.

During this conversation he reminded me of all we meant to each other and how our relationship had progressed. He wanted to assure me that we still had each other; a life together that he cherished and believed would be forgiven in God's eyes.

I asked "How can God forgive us for breaking a commandment?" We have absolutely committed adultery and repeated it many, many times."

Ben winced but said "When I really started to know you I had already sinned with Mrs. Bridgefield, one time, and been caught. That sin was both a punishment and a reward for it led me to you and gave to us both that cherished boy. I will not wish that it had not happened although I certainly wish Mrs. Bridgefield had not lost her life. She might have lived and prospered by having the boy with her but that was not to be. And I will only add this in my own defense; she had been increasingly needy and demanding of my attentions. I had begun to sense that there was a need for me to pull back and perhaps direct her needs to another; you had even given me warning. My trip to her farm that fateful day was to ask her if I might discuss her despair with Deacon Brown's wife, a Godly woman of considerable life experience, by whom I believed she could be comforted."

"But the skies opened up with an unexpectedly harsh storm that afternoon and I could not hold the road with my buggy so fast did the snow accumulate. Thus my return trip, which started as a struggle, ended in my walking the horse back into Mrs. Bridgefield's barnyard. No doubt she was delighted to see me reappear but I felt close to frightened. And as soon as she was able to get her brother and his family out of the main part of her house where they all took meals, she was cornering me. She literally began by pressing herself up against me until I retreated to a corner. Once I was in this corner she stood in front of me but with

her body nearly again against mine. She extended her arm and began caressing my neck and gently touching my ears and face."

"I could be polite no longer and stepped away thinking to propel her back from me while I uttered words to the effect that I was a man of God and a married man. I said loudly that she was pushing us toward adultery. She saw that I was upset; she only laughed and now pressed her entire body against mine. I have never spoken to you of my wife in a critical manner, nor is this an excuse for what happened next, but I must hasten to add that Mrs. Wilbur and I had not enjoyed marital relations since the birth of our last daughter. She always slept next to me at night but so well covered one would think it was below zero in our home. And that is it; she has had zero interest in relations since that time."

"In any case with Mrs. Bridgefield pushing her body against mine and gently stroking my face I felt the male reaction in a way that I know she could not help but feel too. It was then that she took full advantage reaching down and rubbing me in just that area while pressing her lips into mine. The entire situation flashed through my head: no one around, a snowy night in which I was forced to stay and how desperately and incredibly good was this feeling. I must admit to you that this is how weak were my convictions when such a situation presented itself. Why for a split and egotistical second I almost told myself that I was doing the poor widow a service!"

"And then it happened right upon her parlor floor. I burst her bodice open and reveled in what was uncovered and then in an instant I was between her legs, we were surrounded by her petticoats and I was inside her pushing for all I was worth. It was over in just a few moments. I was embarrassed and weak, she appeared joyful and triumphant."

"I staggered out into the snow for a few moments to collect myself and when I came back in she had straightened out the room and was waiting to direct me to a back bedroom for the night. I braced a chair

against the bedroom door to help prevent her return or to at least provide me fair warning if Mrs. Bridgefield did attempt to break in. Then I lay on the bed trembling with fear and guilt and was unable to sleep at all until perhaps an hour or so at dawn. I was fearful of the Lord's judgment but truth be known I was more fearful of Mrs. Wilbur's."

"In any case I remained in this room until I heard the unmistakable tread of her brother's feet in the kitchen. I then assumed some safety based upon this "chaperone" and went out to do what must be done before leaving. He advised that the roads still seemed near impossible to find, never mind to use, but I assured him there seemed to be enough of a lull in the storm that my horse and I would find our way home." "Well" he added, and I think there was a note of sarcasm, "So long as the Lord is with you, Reverend." "I made no reaction to this baiting but hastily took my leave."

"So now Dear Emily you know the sordid details of my sinful, wanton behavior. You also may be angry with me or perhaps better understand why you are so necessary to my life and such a treasure from God. Without you our boy would have known no mother and been kept from his own father. And his father, whether right or wrong would have led a life totally devoid of a woman's love."

"I deeply love and adore my girls and respect their mother but the years I went without the physical love of a woman were very difficult ones. It was harder to keep my focus on the well being of my parishioners when deep down I was so needy myself. I don't know how the Roman Catholic priests manage. And my parents had raised me under strict biblical doctrine. Not only did we not play ball, use cards or dance on the Sabbath but in our everyday lives we did not touch ourselves for pleasure. God forbid I should spill my adolescent seed on the ground! So I lived for those nights when dreams and nature would take control of my body and there could be some physical relief."

"Forgive me Dear Emily if my direct talk is crude or shocking to you. I only want you to see what your love has meant and continues to mean to me. You have been a true wife to me and I cannot bear to have you think that part of our life is over. It cannot be for I still need you so."

17

A SECRET STAIRCASE

*B*en's words were at times shocking and I felt as though too much detail was shared, still they helped me to understand what had gone on between him and Mrs. Bridgefield. I had feared he had a longer relationship with her and therefore bounced back too quickly from her loss, and also bore more guilt, but such was not the case; she had been a predator, the notorious Black Widow Spider which eats its mate. And his affections for Mrs. Wilbur appeared more wrapped in history and oaths than in flesh and blood. He was still a very young man when she had cast him off. What had she expected he would do or did it even matter to her?

I left the Church that day anxious to get home and check on Will but also heartened by Ben's words which portrayed a future as still very possible for us. I entered the kitchen and all was silent. I went down the cellar stairs with a lantern as the side containing Will was rather dim. Not a sound here either but it occurred to me that Will might be rather lonely in this spot. Naturally I spoke to him at length about my day leaving out the sexual parts between his father and biological mother.

Then I explained that Reverend Ben hadn't wanted me sleeping down there with him any longer. That Reverend Ben feared for my health in a damp cellar. So I explained that as he was located just under my bed chamber I would have a set of stairs made running from a trap door starting on the inside of my closet and landing on this very area in the cellar. I promised to keep the trapdoor open all night in case he needed me or slept better when he could hear my breathing.

In this manner I thought to keep Ben from worrying about my mental health as well as the physical and if I ever had any overnight guests they would assume I was fast asleep in my own bed with no access below. I found a farmer just outside of town who promised to build it all very quickly and would not mention it to anyone. As he put it "What goes on in a lady's bedchamber is strictly her business." Now if the Reverend came by at a late hour I could simply close my closet door to "hide the evidence."

There were times when I took to leaving things on the trap door stairs just for Will. One time it was his favorite book about jungle animals and another time his charcoals and sketch pad. Whatever it was had to be woven into the steps in such a way that he could reach them but that the closure of the trapdoor did not simply dump them on the cellar floor; a little tricky but I managed.

When I went back to Church the next day Ben questioned me about how and where I had slept. I could honestly tell him in my own bed and know that soon I would always be there but hopefully not alone.

He began this day by saying of course we had to attend to actual Church matters, but he felt remiss in only talking about himself and his family and what had led up to his fathering Will. He said he believed it was important for us to reminisce about and accept our own behaviors. That our relationship had endured over many years now and we were a family to which he was committed. Did I not feel that with him he asked?

Yes, I promised that I did. I said I had recently realized that women as homely as I were married and had large families so why couldn't what he and I have be real. He said he wished I wouldn't see myself in such a harsh light for the glow of the fire illuminated my inner beauty in his eyes. I was a strong woman, creative even clever, and one who would do the right thing for her partner. He felt certain he could trust me always and that I would stand by him even under the difficult circumstances we had faced. He said I was a wonderful, dear mother to Will. Then he got a twinkle in his eye.

He said he wanted to say this so that I would appreciate what he saw but he didn't wish to cause me pain by saying it awkwardly; he wanted me to know that my form and body were most appealing to him. "You condemn yourself as homely which is far too harsh; any man would be attracted to your figure and your face is lovely," he said. I blushed as though the entire Church choir had just danced naked through the office. But he continued, "Haven't I whispered in your ear the desire I feel when with you? Haven't you believed me?"

I stuttered a bit and then managed to say something to the effect that I had assumed such talk was simply part of the moment but not a true feeling. He said no, that he was in fact quite enamored with me and the necessity of our alliance was the finest part of his life. This pleased as much as shocked me and did have the effect of helping to get me out of a great part of my depression. I thought for a moment he was going to become amorous right there in the Church office but when he drew closer I simply suggested that he might wish to drop me home late afternoon and stop in for tea.

I don't know if it was the sound of our voices mingled together or just the number of days Will had been lying underground but after Ben left my house that evening I went down to the cellar. I had wished to go to him immediately upon returning home but didn't want his father to see more of my behavior which he might judge as unstable. In any case Will had been out and at some point in the day pulled the stairs down and removed his sketch book. I was thrilled to see this sign of activity knowing it meant I was correct about his eminent return to me. For the moment I simply returned the pad to its spot on the stairs and smoothed over the gravesite which Will naturally had been unable to do.

"Perhaps he will speak to me this evening" I thought out loud, just in case he was listening.

18

MINISTERING TO THE ILL

A few days passed and there were no further signs from Will although I checked both morning and night. Yes, I was disappointed but Ben was keeping me so busy with Church business that I really only noticed when I was home utterly alone. Then one morning Ben said he was afraid that he might have another way to complicate my life. I'm certain he meant in addition to having "given me Will".

And what pray tell can this be I asked in rather a lighthearted manner. Ben said he had hoped to avoid ever mentioning this for he felt somehow more disloyal to Mrs. Wilbur by saying anything to anyone but the time had come where it was imprudent NOT to deal with the matter. He added that their oldest daughter, Ginny, was as I knew, in Boston studying and living with his family. The other two girls just managed to handle themselves having been somewhat spared by the hard work of the eldest sister and, of course, their mother. But now their mother, his wife, was fading in a way that made her incapable of managing even her own basic needs. He dreaded to say but she was often incontinent as well as forgetful. She also had developed a tendency to wander which he feared would eventually lead to her getting lost. The girls had to take turns leaving the house so that someone would always be with her and they were expressing resentment of this duty.

My goodness, I said, of course young people like them would find it quite tedious to be tied to an ill parent especially if she appeared well but was troubled in her mind! How sorry I was for all of them. Was there something I might do to help?

Ben said he was thinking of something but needed a bit more time to think it through and speak with the girls. He thanked me for the offer and said he knew he could depend on me to help. As a caution I reminded him that I was now 55 years old and quite an old lady by the calendar even if I did not feel it. He said he had never given my age a thought because I remained so able and so sharp. Then he said that certainly his poor wife would never even live to 55 never mind be capable of managing. He feared her condition might soon be terminal.

Hearing those words I felt rather guilty for the time with him which I had stolen in a sense from her and vowed I would do anything possible to help her. But a few days later, when he asked me to move into their home, taking over Ginny's bedroom, I was stupefied with a sense of loss as this would indeed take away from my possible contacts with Will. Still, I had pledged myself to care for her if I could.

Ben explained that he had spoken at length with Levy and Esther about what went on all day when he was out and to what extent they felt they could still manage the care of their mother. When he brought my name up, mentioning what a caring person I was and how alone I must now be feeling with the loss of my son, they grew excited. "Yes Father, oh please Father, have her live here and then Mother will be safe and we won't have to be so worried." He told them they would still be needed to assist me, that no one person could do all that was now needed to help our Mother from morning to night; to feed her, bathe her, help her with bodily functions and take care that she would do herself no harm. They understood and said they would be so grateful that they would gladly help and would provide me with a schedule of when they could definitely be available.

And so another phase of my life began, one in which I moved into the Parish House in the bedroom of Ginny, their oldest daughter now off to school in Boston. Unusual for a young woman to be so educated but her grandparents were well placed and able to assert that she be treated with deference, indeed, that she was as good as a man! Bravo to them I thought.

I packed a small bag with a few changes of clothing, my books and embroidery; after all my own home was close-by and I wanted reasons to stop there so, in truth, I could check on Will. And really a large farmhouse such as mine always needed attention. Wind could disturb a shingle or water could come down the chimney or a bird or mouse might enter the home and do damage. So the small satchel suited my needs very well.

At first it seemed odd to see Mrs. Wilbur without clothing as was necessitated when bathing her and dressing her. I had never seen my parents without clothing and my brothers were considerably older so it had never happened with them. Ben was the first naked person I had ever seen and he had been a pleasant shock for which my excitement had fairly well prepared me. Then there was my dear baby boy who I loved with every beat of my heart. But another woman without coverings made me embarrassed to the point that I would take a quick look to assess what I must do for her and then I looked away. By so averting my eyes I managed to complete the necessary tasks with only a small bit of distress. I had no idea how she felt as her conversation was increasingly rare and each day made less sense. I took care to always be gentle and to maintain enough banter to distract her from possible unpleasantness.

The girls noted that their mother was now sleeping better which improved the restfulness of the entire house. Ben still slept next to her so that his "night duty" was greatly improved. Although, even by day her trips to the outhouse were decidedly difficult as she didn't always cooperate or manage to hold her water until we could reach the little building. I decided that one way the girls could help without ruining their schedules was to empty, clean and return their mother's chamber pots so that there was always something fresh available. Surprisingly they showed no qualms about so doing and we fell into a reasonable routine of divided labors in a very short time.

It fell to me to make meals but one of them would fetch the needed goods which could be stored in a cool part of their cellar, stored in a cupboard or brought over from the Church where donations were frequently left for Reverend Ben and family. Naturally we gave all possible to poor families but the Rev.'s family had to eat so food replaced what could not be given as salary. My skills in the kitchen, learned at my mother's side, seemed much appreciated.

Part of each day I still devoted directly to the Church. Only when we were alone in the Church did Ben ever say anything personal to me. Within his home he was friendly, even warm, but never loving. Nor did he sneak down the hall late at night when all others might have been sound asleep; within the confines of his home his behavior was exemplary. However, alone in the office we resumed our typical close talking sometimes with amorous overtones and even occasional kisses. When he desired more from me I suggested I might need a buggy ride to my place after we had prepared Mrs. Wilbur for bed and while the girls could look after her. I noted a need for some additional clothing, books or thread. He never questioned this suggestion and so we carried on a healthy yet stealthy love-life within my home.

When he and I were there together I would leave him in the parlor while I "prepared" myself up in my room. What Ben didn't know was that I would make a hasty trip down the stairs via the trapdoor and into the cellar for a chance to see Will. Unfortunately there were never any signs that Will had come out to seek me. Everything would be just as I had left them after he first looked at his sketch book. I wondered if he was angry with me for being gone so much and never being available at night. I would whisper these questions to him but all remained silent.

19

THE PRODIGAL SON

*A*fter about a month of continually sleeping at the Parsonage I began to truly miss my own bed and the comfort of having my own things close by. I thought only slaves, and thank goodness there were none in East Apple, work with nary a day off; perhaps I should ask for a break now and again. In the back of my mind, truth be known, was that I might yet connect with Will if I could sleep at home for a few contiguous days. He was always on my mind and I still could not accept that he was lost to me for the remainder of my earthly life.

So the next morning I made them a particularly good breakfast including sausages which were generally saved for supper. Before Ben could leave for Church and the girls jump-up to do who knows what, I said I needed to make a request of them which I hoped would be tolerable as it was most important to me. Now I had their attention and proceeded to state how dear it was living in their household but I was finding it impossible not to miss some of my routine in my own home. For example I mentioned enjoying a little harvest of my herbs and drying them for teas or garnishes for my cooking. That doing such *things gave me a certain comfort even though the house surely held sad memories. It also held joyous memories too, I added quickly, and housed a few portraits not only of my dear boy but also of my late parents who had meant the world to me.*

The girls were a bit slow in comprehending that I truly wished some time at home for they offered to help harvest my herbs and bring them here to the Parsonage to dry; they also indicated they would love to have Will's portrait about the house and any other paintings which I might hold dear. I thanked them for these kind offers but firmly stated these were but examples of the things I missed about my own home. I said that I did not wish to be away for long and would not abandon them with the duties required to care for their mother but perhaps could I have three days off and then build three days a month off into the schedule for future months?

Ben replied immediately that they had all been too selfish and had not considered my needs adequately as this arrangement was so beneficial to them. Of course I could have what time I needed for myself and he would give more time to his wife as he should, that I should not worry. I thanked him and asked when I might take those first three days away as I felt the need. He asked if the next day would be soon enough so that he could first tidy up a few things at the office. I replied that certainly it was and likely I would stop in the office today while Mrs. Wilbur was napping and help him to prepare. I also suggested that during my days off from the Parsonage I would still be available for some Church duties. And just like that it was settled!

I spent that last night in the Parsonage, prepared a simple meal for breakfast, and then Ben kindly drove me with my satchel to the Rattlesnake Hill Road home. As we traveled he asked calmly if my need to be home had anything to do with my former inclination of sleeping next to Will's grave. I was not in the habit of lying to Ben but this was a difficult subject for us. I told him the things I had mentioned the previous night while talking with the girls were all true and important to me. I left it at that. He cleared his throat and then said, "Very well but please be careful as you are most precious to me." I replied "Don't worry Ben this is just a little hiatus for me. I will be fine; and you remain very precious to me."

Ben helped me carry my things into the house and he did a bit of a walk around the interior to be certain nothing seemed amiss. Once he was satisfied as to my safety he held me a moment and kissed me good-bye. I again assured him I'd be in the Church Office first thing the next morning. He smiled and was on his way. I stood near the window watching him go just long enough to be sure he wouldn't turn back for something, and then I rushed down the cellar stairs.

Per usual of late there was no sign from, or of, Will. All was quiet and the trapdoor appeared undisturbed. I stood next to the spot in the cellar floor which held him and said "Will, it is mother. I know I have been gone much of the time but Rev. Ben is in dire need of help with Mrs. Wilbur. With Ginny off to Boston the two younger girls were having difficulty managing their mother well enough to keep their father free to work. They desperately needed my help. I thought about you every moment and checked in here whenever I could. I am so sorry if you needed me but I shall remain here for 3 nights and longer if you need me to. Just please dear Will, let me know. I'll have the stairs down tonight and the closet door to my room wide open. I love you and miss you dear."

Emotionally exhausted I climbed the cellar stairs to the kitchen. I wanted to look in the cupboards for any pickled beets and pickled green beans I might have. A couple of cured smoked hams hung on hooks in the kitchen so I knew I could eat that night, and for many days should I have a need. Levy had wrapped some bread for me and placed a half dozen eggs and a large slice of cheese in paper tucked into a sack for my short trip home. I was really just trying to keep busy until Will wanted to communicate. I was counting on hearing something that night.

I put aside the wedding portrait of my parents to make good on my claim of missing seeing this. Now I would place it by my bedside on the table at the Parsonage. I also went to my room and removed the small painting of Will from that wall. Perhaps Ben would be good enough to hang it for me wherever they didn't mind having a hook. Then I swept and dusted to keep down any dirt and, dare I say, "spider-webs". I aired the house out and resealed the windows before eating my meal and settling into bed.

Once in my room I opened the closet door, allowed the trapdoor to hang down and called to Will that I was now going to bed. With the lantern burning in my window, for any passerby to see, I sat in bed trying to read; thoughts of Will ruined my concentration such that I reread the same paragraph four times before having a clue as to what was its content. Finally I gave up and extinguished the lantern followed by a restless sleep interrupted by every creak of the boards or acorn that fell on the roof. Eventually this dozing led into morning and I awoke having heard nothing from Will.

Still the first thing I did upon rising was to check on him by running down the trapdoor steps and calling his name. I was met by silence, no sign of dirt that had been disturbed, and no evidence that his objects had been enjoyed. I was crestfallen but went about my business washing for the day, cooking my eggs and dressing for the Church Office. I decided to walk briskly to make up for being a bit slow this morning.

The farmer who had recently done the closet/cellar carpentry work happened by headed for the center of town with a load of hay on his wagon probably going to the Town Stable. Surely they must have to purchase food and bedding for their animals from someone like him. He asked if I wanted a ride to Church. I thanked him kindly but said no, I needed the exercise. What I was thinking was that he already knew too much about my business and I did not wish to answer any questions he might pose.

Ben welcomed me with obvious joy and asked how I was doing. I in turn asked about the girls and especially Mrs. Wilbur's health. All appeared normal so I went right to work. It was then that Ben came and stood behind me apparently waiting for me to look up. After a moment I said "Yes Reverend?" in a good-natured manner. His concern was to be certain that I was truly okay and still planning to return to the Parsonage to live after another two nights at my own house. I assured him I planned to return and then asked if he would mind coming with the carriage for me in the morning two days hence; that would allow me to bring my two portraits along with my satchel, leave these items at the Parsonage and still be at work on time on that morning. Of course that request was fine with him and seemed to reassure him.

That evening I again spoke with Will, or rather the mound in the cellar. I implored him to take action to speak with me as I was only there at night for this night and one more before returning to the Reverend Ben's house. I then went about my business drying a few more herbs and cleaning two smoky windows in the kitchen. At night fall I repeated all I had done the previous evening complete with a call down from the trapdoor that I was now going to bed.

Sadly the result by next morning was much the same; a restless sleep and no word or actions from Will. I felt close to tears and had to fight them throughout my walk to Church. Being both tired and disappointed made cheerfulness and high spirits difficult to find this morning which I think Ben sensed for he held me for a few moments and asked no questions. A parishioner had called for Ben late afternoon. It seemed his mother-in-law was dying and wished to speak with the Minister. Naturally Ben obliged but as he was leaving he turned back and, closing *the door again for a moment of privacy with me, said "I feel that you are in pain. Please remember that I love you and I will come by for you first thing in the morning." He then left so as not to arouse any concern in the man who awaited him.*

This brought back the tears. I pulled myself together and left for home. It was a bit early but this would be my last night there for several weeks based on the agreement we had made. I was anxious to give Will one more opportunity to reach me.

Again I went to the cellar and spoke at length to my dear boy imploring him to please make contact as I missed him so fiercely. I hurried through my chores and the small bit of packing I needed to do for the morning. I washed early and arrived in my bedchamber with extra time for sleep or the talking for which I longed. As usual I opened up the trapdoor and notified my son that I was there, and then I climbed into bed to read and wait.

I don't know exactly what time it was as I must have been so exhausted that I finally dropped off to sleep but I heard a dull scratching sound like a cat in a sandbox. It went on for several minutes. Inexplicably I felt unable to move as though I had starched myself into the sheets and they would not release me. Then I heard a groan as though someone in pain was struggling to move forward followed by a tread on the stairs; one that sounded much like a leg was being dragged along. I recognized that someone or something was moving towards me. I struggled to fully awaken feeling a chill throughout my bones and a sense of intense fear, no, it was terror. But before I could even manage to get out of my bed a vile appearing creature stood before me right there in the closet doorway. He was facing me. The area was lit faintly by the moon yet there could be no question that I had to acknowledge this creature was Will. Will was actually standing before me!

And what I beheld was a true horror. His ashen skin was hanging from his face and hands, there were two giant spiders clinging to him, and his breath was worse than anything imaginable; it seemed a mixture of earth from the bottom of the outhouse with the sickening odor of an animal long dead in the woods and calling to flies. I could not help but gag and gasp.

"Is this what you wanted to see mother?" he seemed to sneer. "Did you wish to see me as I decompose?" he asked with an angry tremor. "Grotesque am I not? Now Mother you must leave me alone! Annabella and her children lie in rest with me. They were to sleep for 100 years before returning but thanks to your insistence I was granted this visit only at a price. We must all lie dormant for another 100 years doubling our time of rot. I will be back mother but you will be long gone by the year 2020 or close to then when we are released. The children will appear first to prepare the world. Yet if this house stands I shall again walk its halls and visit with its people. But you must now allow us to lie in peace. Go live and ask no more of me I beg of you. I would smile and hug you goodbye but my lips no longer obey me and I fear the stench would overwhelm you so farewell dear Mother." It was impossible to determine if these last words were spoken from heartbreak or anger but their effect only enhanced my horror. Yet as he began to turn I was certain I saw a single tear slide down what was left of his once beautiful countenance.

With that he turned completely away and descended the stairs sending the ladder back up with a loud crash. This helped to break the spell in which I was trapped. My stomach was presenting an unmanageable problem and I rushed to the chamber pot where I would wretch off and on for the remainder of the night. In between the bouts of illness I listened at my closet door but could hear nothing. I tried returning to bed and was able to rest for only a few minutes at a time; it seemed the smell would not leave the room.

When I saw first morning light I opened all curtains and windows in my room to help circulate some air. I took the chamber pot outside *and washed it. I washed myself and left my night clothing to soak in a tub. I wept uncontrollably for a few minutes then forced myself to pull together and placed cold cloths upon my face, combed my hair and dressed for the day. I was unable to eat anything but sucked on some mint leaves which seemed to soothe my stomach. There was still time before Ben should arrive so I determined to take a quick walk into the cellar.*

I stepped down the staircase off the kitchen and was surprised at how cool was the atmosphere and how I sensed no unusual odor. I hesitantly made my way to his gravesite expecting to see all manner of horrible things including spiders and flies; but I found nothing. Nothing at all: Even the dirt was as smooth as it had been when last I put things in order. I dared not speak but made my way back up the cellar stairs and into the kitchen. Was it possible that this had been a dream? Yet, I recalled the stench and my illness so vividly. It makes a dream quite unlikely.

I felt shaky and feared I might faint although I have never been a "fainting" type of person. I drank a glass of water which sat on the counter, gathered my bags and the portraits and sat down near a window to wait for Ben.

20

A PROPOSAL

When Ben helped me into the wagon with my things he seemed very cheerful. His deep sadness over his wife and our loss of Will seemed mitigated by being able to count on me. This thought began to defrost my heart and soul after the night of terror. I managed to smile but my conversation was so tentative and flat that he recognized immediately that I was in crisis. He was so kind and solicitous of my needs that I could not hold back the truth even though my thought had been to conceal the story.

When I finished reviewing the details of the night he was holding my hand but down low in the wagon where no passer-by could observe such a thing. We were both teary; well Ben was teary and I had again begun sobbing. He asked me if I had slept or eaten. I explained how troubled my stomach now was and said I had slept early in the night but probably not since two or three this morning. He wondered if I wished to sleep at the Parsonage for a few hours to get my strength back and return to the Office tomorrow. I allowed that sounded nice but I feared *being apart from him just now and it wouldn't look right for him to stay home and care for me.*

We agreed that I'd go leave my things off and then we would arrive together at the Church. He made me repeat the part of the story where I found no evidence this morning of the actions from the grave last night. He asked if I could possibly have been so anxious and determined to see Will that my inner mind had taken over and I had dreamt the entire appearance of Will. I said I had asked myself that very question but didn't think so and that cleaning the chamber pot was real enough. Ben said he was sure that was real but that the mind can cause physical illness under harsh enough circumstances. "Well," he added, "we'll give this time and see how you feel on the morrow."

And so I bluffed my way through the short stop at the Parsonage so that the girls would detect nothing amiss and I dutifully went off to the Church with the Reverend. Twenty-four hours later that home, my safe-haven, would be torn by grief yet again and I would move to a loft room so that Ginny could return from Boston. Mrs. Wilbur could not be awakened in the morning and the doctor determined that she had perished in her sleep probably from some type of blood abnormality. At any rate she was suddenly and totally gone from their lives.

I did all I could to stay in the background and care for the family and those that would visit. In truth the Church members did most of the food preparation and I had only to coordinate the keeping and distribution of the items. Ben was distraught but more for his daughters at this point; and he was concerned when I suggested I would go home after the funeral was over. I said it would not look good if a single woman was living with a widower. His opinion was that I would be living with a widower and two or three daughters to help them manage their home. I repeated his words to give it time and 'we would see on the morrow'.

After about three weeks I convinced him to let me sleep again in my own home and continue to work in the Church Office with a few stops each week at the Parsonage to see that they could manage things. I also asked him to come to my cellar with me when he left me off while I made my first check on things since the morning after the incident. As we walked into my house he stopped me and said "Emily as soon as a few months have passed I would like you to become my wife."

Ben said he had a plan to retire as Pastor in just a few more years, once all three girls were married or had attained the age of 18. He would love to continue helping with the Church and with me by his side it would be a pleasure. He also said he'd enjoy becoming a gentleman farmer if that suited me. He reminded me that the Parsonage belonged to the congregation and that any new Pastor would live there so he and I could live out our lives on Rattlesnake Hill Road in my farmhouse, he paused a moment, then added "with Will."

21

EMILY'S WARNING

A s I continued to read from Emily's Diary I was certainly struck by her deep love for this child and for Reverend Benjamin Wilbur. Within this part of the Diary I found a note in a tattered and fragile envelope that was more yellowed than white in color. It was addressed to "The Owner of the Wilbur-Harrison Estate on Rattlesnake Hill Road" so, I guessed, apparently they did marry and share the property as their names were combined. I gently opened the epistle hoping it would not deteriorate in my hands before being able to reveal its secrets. The handwriting within was lovely and looping in a faded and thin black ink, just the style I had been reading in the Harrison Diaries so I felt certain this was a letter from Emily to me.

The statement within was simple and direct. It read: "There should be a large white stone behind your house. It bears a message of which you ought to take heed especially should you happen upon it on or around the years of 2020 to 2022. Within this time these words are intended for you. Trust the stone's meaning." Then the words on the stone were repeated:

Wilbur Harrison, beloved son, 1811 – 1823
Shed not for him a single tear
Spare not for him your regret
'Tis but the body that lies here
The soul that graced it
Wanders yet!

Now I had the full name which had been nearly worn off the gravestone. And I searched the poem desperate to finally understand its meaning. Was it no accident that I had found this? It seemed only the last two lines could be a caution for which I must be alert. Did his soul now wander? Was Emily mentioning these dates because they correspond with the times she had predicted Will and Annabella would be back? And had not the giant arachnids nearly destroyed our exterminator Peter this year, 2019? Was this a sign that more was yet to come? If Annabella and her children had been alive in our cellar was Will too then among the living?

These were frightening questions for which I felt I must determine the answers and quickly! I told Fred about this disturbing note.

He said "Just 'cause you find an old message like that don't make it true. Folks back then had a lot of weird superstitious ideas I wouldn't give a hoot for."

"Yes," I replied, "but this one was even chiseled in stone." Fred found that amusing but it didn't have much effect on his opinion of the veracity of the information. He didn't think I should get all hot and bothered over a 200 year old note. And certainly he wasn't volunteering to take a shovel down to the packed cellar floor and begin trying to loosen the soil for an exhumation. I had to agree that finding spiders, even gigantic ones, in an old cellar was quite a different matter than finding a 200 year old twelve year old boy! Still I did not feel I could justifiably ignore a warning such as this one.

I called Pastor Martin to see if he had ever read the note. "No", was the response, he claimed never to have been aware of it. He did note that Reverend Wilbur had married Miss Harrison about a year after his wife and Miss Harrison's son had died. Shortly thereafter the Reverend had retired from his calling to the Church and became a simple parishioner. He and the new Mrs. Wilbur had taken well to the agrarian life although Mrs. Wilbur was at least fifty-five by this point. Records show their place was reasonably prosperous; they raised sheep and had a good income from blueberry and apple farming; it was also noted that they kept chickens and herbs for personal use.

"His oldest daughter, known as Ginny," Reverend Martin continued, "remained in Boston most of her life having married a sea captain, Captain Benner, and herself working at a university. The other two girls stayed locally but were also both married. The middle one, Levy, now Mills, had three sons and named one after Will, her father and Miss Harrison's foundling. Of course another was named Ben for her dad, and there youngest was Theodor. Apparently she and her family spent a good deal of time with her father and Emily. Emily had done much to help them out as children when their mother was ill, and Emily also adored playing the role of grandmother to Esther's four girls. Esther had married a man named John Farmer who was indeed, a farmer."

"The Reverend lived to be seventy-eight years old, quite an elderly fellow for those times; and Emily lived to be nearly one hundred. Shortly before her death, she had gotten a little soft in the head if you know what I mean; she claimed she just needed to last another one hundred plus years for her dreams to come true. No one quite understood what she meant although she had a weird poem inscribed on her late son's tombstone which was now installed in her backyard. In any case, Esther, who cared for her and lived on Emily's farm along with her husband and their two youngest daughters, apparently paid no attention to it."

I asked him if he thought that note, which highlighted the message on the tombstone, was important to me in this time 200 years after Will's passing. He said he could not imagine how it would be. "Just the fanciful mind of an elderly lady is my thought" was his reply. I thanked him and moved on.

I next called the State Trooper who had been looking for our 'backyard camper'. He had promised to keep us informed of Joseph's location, especially if Joseph left Kentucky. The response was that Joseph had never turned up back here but if he did return to the area they would at least question him. They had been told that he went to Kentucky to live with his parents and assumed I'd hear nothing more from him. I decided to check with the college kids next door to see if the "haunting" they were experiencing had ended or not. At least we had no more missing items or strange groaning. I hoped that this all turned out well. Since I knew whose tombstone we had, and the haunting issues had ceased, I now just had to be certain that Matt was feeling better about his research. Once all these things resolved we could then be in pretty good shape to continue plans for a baby.

22

AWARDING OF TENURE

Matt had asked me to help with the final stages of his major manuscript. He had numbered all his footnotes in the body of the paper but had not had the computer function to produce the bibliography. My guess was he had taken shortcuts in recording details which at the last moment I would be hunting for and compiling according to American Psychological Association guidelines. Being meticulous with this bibliography was essential for the journals he wished to have accept his work. Nothing was worse than having unsubstantiated or unreferenced concepts that one then built their theories upon. He could be thought careless or, worse still, judged to be fraudulent.

While this was a tedious task I was pleased to do it for him just as I had done for his dissertation. Someone said the spouse of any professor has probably also earned a doctorate. I didn't want credit for anything but took pride in my contribution and hoped he would soon be able to relax and enjoy the life we were building. I did wonder why his graduate assistant wasn't doing more of this work but didn't want to introduce any potentially touchy subjects.

I was also assisting him in designing his final tables to demonstrate the results of their study on multiple personality disorder. These findings seemed to indicate that a number of people legitimately were leading at least two separate lives, each one, for there could be several, unaware of the others. Matt seemed excited at having attained these results although they were replicating older research.

In any case by late summer the research projects were already submitted. Matt had done something especially clever; as it was his tenure year and he needed to be able to state what would be published and where, he had gotten a "preliminary-acceptance" letter from two of the journals. Based upon his data summary they agreed to accept his articles if submitted by a certain date. No wonder he was under extreme pressure. And Matt was overjoyed the day he went in to submit three articles electronically followed by hard copies going immediately in the mail.

We were eating a feast of celebration, just about to clink our champagne glasses, when his Dean called. It seemed the Tenure Committee Chair had come to the Dean with a problem. Matt's graduate assistant was filing a complaint that his name should appear as first author on one of those Tenure-needed publications. That Matt was trying to steal the student's intellectual property! Matt set the phone down and looked dazed. I yelled "I know how much you have dedicated yourself to this work and he's got to be nuts! What's his game?"

Matt said, "He could possibly be retaliating for the night I was too harsh with him and caused him embarrassment. Or maybe he wants a grade change for his summer course. I don't know."

"Who would accuse their major adviser of such a thing over something that should be settled in a discussion?" I exclaimed.

Matt said, "There is only one way to find out but the University has already appointed a committee of three to review it all so I shouldn't just call him up. The committee will now be fact-finding."

"What does that mean for your tenure?" I asked. Nearly saying what does it mean for our future.

Matt seemed pretty calm and explained that; "The University would try to be as expeditious as possible so my future should not be on hold for very long." But, he added, if he lost this "squabble" it would result in denial of tenure and therefore loss of his job. The student could always claim a misunderstanding so he had little to lose. I just kept thinking 'why?'

The next day I was on campus looking at some historical photos to see if we wanted to have our barn updated to look like one in the old Agricultural College. There were numerous barns to review and all would be in keeping with the time period of our home. The problem was that our barn currently was a bit of an amalgamation of the original structure with stalls, lean-tos, woodsheds and entire wings having been added. I wondered if we should simply go back to the original form or save some of these additions and if so in what configuration. No matter how much space we had I hated to give any up always thinking that someday I might want to open an herb shop or have a studio; or Matt might want a work shed or perhaps we'd have a playroom for our future children. There were endless possibilities yet simultaneously our primary concern was the aesthetic of the design and relevancy to the time period in which the house had been built.

It was certainly exciting to be at this point in the renovations. Choosing colors and styles along with wallpaper, sinks, tubs and faucets was far more fun than scraping and sanding had been.

Decorating solid walls was far more enjoyable than dealing with cracks and leaks – the house and carpenters had come a long way with much thanks to Fred. The modern plumbing was our major concession to the current century but wherever possible we chose old style items, for example, we had a sink placed inside the top of an antique dresser and the shower hidden around the corner in that bathroom so you weren't confronted with 'modern' as you walked into the room.

I was just finishing up my review of barns when I noticed the time was already afternoon. It made sense to me to stop at the University cafeteria for a quick bite to eat. I went in, grabbed a tuna fish sandwich, some chips and a diet coke and sat myself at the nearest vacant table. Within five minutes Terry, Matt's graduate assistant walked over and pulled out a chair. He was a nice looking young man wearing a short sleeved shirt bearing a small red and black checked pattern, khaki pants and loafers; kind of a teaching assistant look if ever there was one.

I had no time to protest his joining me although red flashes went off in my head about us being on different sides of a legal matter. I said "Nice to see you Terry but I'm not sure we should be meeting like this." To which he replied "I'm not going to say anything about the suit, I just want to stay friendly."

Without thinking what I was about to say I responded honestly, "How can you hope to stay friendly when you are trying to ruin my husband's career after he carried you for months with his grant money?" Then I reflexively covered my mouth and said, "Sorry I shouldn't have said that."

Terry replied, "Well maybe we should talk. I found hundreds of references for him he would have overlooked. I highlighted the most salient findings for him to quote, and I compared and contrasted his results with those from the seventies and earlier. His article would have been flat without my help!"

"Look, Terry," I interjected, "we both know that the idea for the study was his, he designed the hypothesis and the study itself and hired you to help do the things you just described. In fact his doctoral dissertation was on this topic so this study is an offshoot from that work. Why would you sue him for first authorship? I just don't get it!"

His response was somewhat pathetic: "I agreed to do the work he outlined and I went above and beyond what should have been sufficient. I happily grant him the first two primary authorships but we had never said he would get three articles out of this research. He needs to share and I worked very hard. Also I'm just starting to break into the world of the academic, moving beyond my role as a student. I thought the whole point of my assistantship was to encourage my forward progress!"

"Terry" I said, barely restraining myself from shaking him, "the way you get to be an academic initially is just the way you and Matt had planned things; you ride his coattails into the journals which currently recognize and respect his name, and then your original work will be deemed meritorious in the future and will be published because your name is on it. But first things first! He gets tenure and you complete your doctorate with his guidance but you are first author on all publications generated from your dissertation. Matt's publications, with you as second author, will be on your Curriculum Vita and only help strengthen your credentials. After that you get a job and start instructing your own students."

I continued on a roll but trying not to shout at him. "You were still making research errors while conducting these studies as Matt had to point out to you; you aren't quite ready yet. And furthermore don't you realize that your first jobs in academia will require a reference letter from your major advisor? What will you say at your job interviews, if you get interviews, when they ask for letters of support from Dr. Nelson? It is always anticipated that your major advisor is your chief 'supporter' and paving the way for your success!" Terry looked stunned then crestfallen. "I guess I hadn't thought this all the way through. I expected immediate results and so had my folks."

"With time, Terry, with time," I uttered then gathered up my sandwich, chips and soda and forced them into my pocketbook. "I've got to run now but please think about what we've discussed this afternoon and let the Dean know if you've reconsidered your position." He rose slightly from his chair and said "Thank you I will." Somehow I felt as though he had accepted a new view and I hoped for the best.

Later that afternoon Terry did go to the Dean, asked for an appointment, and by 10AM the next day had withdrawn his accusation against Matt. Word was he continued to grumble about all he had done for Matt but was no longer filing a formal complaint. Matt would be in a delicate situation when the time came to act as Terry's reference but at least the Promotion and Tenure Committee could review Matt within the normal limits of the Fall semester. Matt confided that he would especially have difficulty in describing Terry as a team player or as a skilled researcher which is what the Ph.D. was supposed to stand for but we both breathed easier with this surprise hurdle removed. And by Christmas Eve the house was nearly brought up to our standard for a reliable and attractive historical home, the stockings were hung by the chimney and the Provost had signed the letter of support for Matt's Tenure. All that remained was the March meeting of the Board of Trustees which would make it final. That vote was to occur on March 13, 2020.

23

2019 DRAWS TO AN END

Late in 2019 I was collecting unwanted boards and general debris out of the main barn. This was about to be renovated so that animals or gardening supplies could be housed safely within these old walls. Wedged between a partly framed door, then filled in with scrap materials, I thought I caught sight of a metal box similar to a vault box. I positioned myself to have a closer look and uncovered what indeed was a strongbox of sorts. I tried the release button almost before I fully retrieved it but found it was securely locked. It was about 8" by 12" and probably originally gray but now considerably scratched. The metal felt thick and, along with its contents, must have weighed five or six pounds. I brought it out of the barn and set it on a stone wall to consider the possible ways of opening it while doing the least damage to the box. I believed this container, on our property, was then our property but still did not want to destroy it.

In the sunlight the lock stuck up from the lid about a quarter of an inch. If I held the box on its side I might well strike the lock a glancing blow and release it. I left it on the wall and hunted around for our hammer. Once the hammer was located I steadied the box and took a strong swing at the lock. Naturally my first blow missed and my arm shook for a few moments from the force of hitting rock so solidly. When I recovered from this I concentrated more and my next strike was successful! I could feel the inner mechanism give way and the lock seemed to pop.

I then sat on the wall and pulled the lid up from its fitting. Inside I found three baby teeth preserved in some kind of waxy substance, a Christian cross on a delicate chain that appeared appropriate for a child. The chain was, in fact, broken and knotted in two other places. It must have been a silver chain but was now so tarnished that it was badly blackened. There was also a mouse bitten printed sheet of paper which appeared to have a picture of a church on it. My guess based on the few words I could make out was that it was the church program from Will's Christening. This must have been a box of treasures that Emily held dear.

The bulk of the space and the real weight in the box were the many sheets of paper it held. It appeared they had been tied together with a ribbon and then wrapped several times in a piece of cotton. Perhaps it had been a gingham print but most of it no longer bore color and the ribbon fell apart in my fingers. The writing however was quite legible and unmistakably that of Emily. The cover page, for that is how this began, said "Life After the Death of Wilbur Harrison" by Emily Harrison and was set up more like a manuscript than a diary. I had felt certain she would continue to record her thoughts and feelings about his life and loss and that of her new life as Ben's wife. How exciting to find the document.

At that point I was interrupted by a honking at the end of the driveway. I looked down the side of the property and there was the mail delivery van apparently needing my attention. I dashed down front not wishing to hold anyone up and the post woman said "I think someone's playing a dirty trick on you?"

"What gives?" I replied. "Well she said, holding a box at arm's length, there has been a decidedly unpleasant smell in the truck all morning and you're almost my last delivery and this package appears to be the culprit." At which point she gave the container a brief sniff, wrinkled up her nose, and held the box in question towards me.

As I drew closer I had to admit it was giving off a disgusting odor like rotting flesh. She said that thought had crossed her mind. If I wouldn't mind opening it in front of her, she said, she would like to report it to the Post Master should it be some kind of a hoax or a danger. And if it was simply a gift gone wrong she would like to know who sent it and when; also what had they been told to expect about the possible length of the delivery process.

And so I proceeded, with all due caution, to rip the paper packing material off and lift the cover. The closer I got to the insides of the box the worse was the stench. When the cover was removed I had to pull away from the box and travel several feet in order to gulp fresh air. But before I had jumped back from the box I had clearly seen a mangled rat rotting inside. "What the heck" I shouted feeling very wounded but not wishing to be crude in front of the delivery woman.

She took a picture of the contents then I got a pitchfork from the barn and removed the dead rodent to an unused section of the property. She wanted to keep the box and all packaging materials together in a garbage-like bag she had with her. She asked if we had any enemies and I said I could think of no one who would do such a thing. Then she asked if our friends had weird senses of humor to which I replied "Yes, but they are funny not gross." She wanted to clarify and have me state directly that I did not know who had sent this to us. I was able to so state.

Together we inspected the address label. There was no return address but a bit of hasty looking scribbling where an address might have appeared. Perhaps it was there to keep a blank corner from drawing attention to the fact that there was no return address. In any case the package did not appear to harbor any clues regarding who had sent it and as to why it was sent. However, the box was addressed to Dr. and Mrs. Matthew Nelson so whoever didn't like us didn't like both of us. Certainly I, being the one who works at home, would also be the one to retrieve the mail and find the package. And in this heat the box would be in no condition to be left for opening when Matt gets home.

I started asking myself had I been rude to a workman. Had we failed to pay someone in a timely fashion? Had we backed out on someone badly needing work? Each question was quickly answered with a "no" until I got to a question about Matt making any enemies at his job. And the only real difficulty Matt had we believed was resolved when Terry had changed his attitude and withdrawn his suit. But could he have simply withdrawn the suit out of political prudence and practicality but not changed his attitude?

Still I didn't wish to make our possible issues with Terry a Federal offense which anything with the Postal Service would be. I simply denied any knowledge of the origins of the delivery saying I would check with my husband upon his return that evening and one of us would call the Postal Authority in the morning. I thanked her for her extra effort on our behalf and apologized for the unknown person or persons who had caused us all this annoyance.

She seemed convinced that whoever did this was very intentional in "his" behavior and cautioned me to keep considering the possibilities.

Also, she was saying, we should have our guard up as this first disgusting act might not be the last. What flashed before me were scenes from movies where the family animals had not made out so well. There was a pet cat or some small animal in a stew pot in one notable scene in Fatal Attraction and the head of a prize race horse found in its owner's bed in The Godfather. I decided that Sybil should stay in the house for the next few weeks and it was definitely time to introduce our dog, Scruffy, to this property.

Scruffy had remained away until a pen was built for him and there were no longer workman constantly coming in and out of the place. His friendliness would only have hindered progress but the fact that he liked to bark whenever he heard an unexplained noise would now serve as a warning. It would be good to have him home for Christmas.

That evening Matt and I made a plan to go on the weekend and retrieve our dog. We also wracked our brains hoping to dislodge some thought as to who sent the grotesque mailing. We did wonder if the Macintoshes' son would have mailed such a thing. The postal marking was local and he had recently been seen in our woods but then subsequent reports placed him back in Kentucky. This led us back to suspecting Terry. "But if it was Terry," I protested, "why didn't he just stick it in our mailbox and keep on driving? Why take a chance on being detected by bringing it into the Post Office?"

"He probably mailed the box before it started to decompose and give off any odor knowing that the weather would do the rest of the job" replied Matt. "And if he had actually delivered it to our mailbox himself any passerby might have noticed someone not in a postal delivery vehicle using the US mailbox. Out here in the country neighbors have a way of noticing pretty much everything", he added.

So we decided that Matt would call the authorities in the morning and suggest that they might wish to question Terry Plotus to see if he knew anything about the "rat coffin" we had received. Matt said he'd be certain to be very tentative and to be clear with them that we did not believe this suggestion was a strong possibility, just a vague inkling.

Out of nowhere we heard pounding on the kitchen ell door around seven o'clock the next evening. There was still daylight but as we weren't expecting anyone it made us jump. Matt answered the door and said "No, please Terry, come right in." I looked up rather surprised.

Terry stood there clearly with adrenaline pumping hard as his veins stood out in both his arms and his neck and his face was flushed. His jaw was extended and he was breathing through his mouth almost as though he had run here rather than driven. There was just a hint of his shaking and he seemed to clench up even more to speak. His words were just as fiery as was his body language. "What the hell did you accuse me of this time?" he spewed in our direction.

"Now look Terry" Matt began in a soothing rather than hostile tone, "we had to tell the Postal Authority if we had any, absolutely any, bad relationship with someone local as they are trying to investigate a seriously offensive package we received. In no way did we say it WAS from you, just that you are the only person with whom I was at odds in recent months. In fact we said we did NOT think you would do such a thing but you COULD possibly have done this in a weak moment."

I just sat at the dinner table with my eyes wide open in utter astonishment and a mixture of fear. I was darn glad Matt was home that evening as this confrontation would have been even more alarming for me alone. Terry continued, "Well what the fuck is it

I'm even supposed to have done here, they never actually stated the crime?"

"It was a crime because the Postal Service was used for a horrible prank by someone", I managed to stammer out. Then I described the gross dead and rotting rat to him. By the time I finished using every adjective I knew to say "disgusting" I had started laughing. Then I said it wasn't funny and apologized but then I started laughing some more. I guess I was demonstrating a mild hysteria. Thank goodness it was contagious because after a couple of minutes Terry started to laugh too and then Matt relaxed enough to join us.

"So you guys aren't pressing charges on me or anything like that?" Terry asked. "No" we assured him, just trying to get to the bottom of a sick prank that really upset our mail carrier we said. "And actually me too at the time" I added. "But it must have been harmless although I don't get it, or who we know with that sense of sinister humor" I concluded. "If our names hadn't been on the package I would have presumed it was intended for a former resident."

After he left we both felt badly about even having supplied his name to the Postal Service. We felt certain, although he had a history of making errors calling his judgment into question, that Terry was not a cruel or sadistic practical joker. But it appeared whoever that "joker" was they were not yet finished with us for later that night we were awakened by debris being hurled at the house.

Again we were both awakened from a dead sleep. The alarm clock read 2 AM, and on and around our bedroom windows, down the hall and on the floor below, we heard the heavy sound of an object hitting the house and then popping. We scrambled out of bed and ran down the stairs throwing on our exterior lights but not before the culprit or culprits were gone. Definitely a car drove off but we were unable to clearly see it or catch the number of the license plate.

There were no holes in the windows or broken shards of glass on the floor so we decided to face this squarely in the morning. Daylight revealed minor rock damage and oozed and drying eggs running down our newly installed windows and our fresh paint. Egging, is a nasty mess but within the margins of prank behavior; the State Troopers said they would not come out on a call at that level.

So for the next three nights Matt and I took shifts sitting in the dark on our porch with a finger on a switch that would light up the front of our house like a 4th of July celebration. Hardly a car passed by and those that did were not slowing down; they gave no appearance of considering an attack. All was quiet. Given that it was fairly cool out there while waiting for trouble, and our electric blankets only accomplished a little, we easily convinced ourselves to stay in bed on the fourth night.

That is precisely when the next attack came. "Pow, pow, crack, crack" and we were wide awake and trying to illuminate the property again. This time I had a camera ready and Matt had a shot gun filled with rock salt that a farmer friend had said scares birds without hurting them, but our reaction time was not good enough. Our frustration level was high, our just washed windows were again covered in yolk and we could not get back to sleep.

This was repeated on several other evenings and then it simply went away. We took heart after a quiet week, retrieving our dog, cleaning everything until it was shining and then hanging wreathes on the windows for the holiday season. We still had not a notion of why we had been selected for this treatment but I did remember back to an encounter I had with a long term neighbor who lived across from Priscilla.

On the first really hot day of the spring, just before we were going to purchase the house, I had seen a woman out in her yard pushing a few weeds around with a hoe. The kind of day you wish would mean nature was totally ready for summer but which all New Englanders knew would invariably be followed by another snow. In any case she had on a straw hat, flip-flops and a black bathing suit. I thought perhaps she would welcome meeting a new neighbor and might have plenty to say; in any case I might enjoy her apparent eccentricity.

I pulled into her large yard not too far from where she was working. I introduced myself and she said she was Edith Bancroft. She spoke with her head held high and in such a manner that I was certain she must have expected me to be impressed by the name. Even though I am a woman I was frankly having a difficult time not staring at her body. She was undoubtedly over sixty and had a considerable weight problem the bulk of which was in her chest. The straps on the top of her bathing suit were under enormous pressure and I marveled that they were holding her considerable bosom up. I was afraid to ask a question for fear of her taking in a breath of air and then exploding open! Where would I run?

But there was one saving grace; something I had not noticed from the road was her necklace which appeared to consist of large rubies and pearls. I found that if I kept my eyes on the gems then I could avoid seeing too much of her flesh and perhaps avoid having nightmares. She continued to speak. "Colonel Bancroft and I have lived here for years and raised our family in this enormous house. Of course the children are gone now so we've taken to renting the rooms out but no kitchen privileges and no hotplates in your rooms. Most students simply take their meals at the University."

I smiled and said that my husband, who was on the faculty, and I would be purchasing the old Harrison place down the hill from her so we weren't in the market for a rental but it was nice to know that things were available should his students express a need. I was just attempting to meet as many neighbors as I might and wondered how she liked the street.

"Oh," she lit up probably as Matt too had a title, "wasn't that a nice idea. We had been very content here for the first twenty years or so but we think someone, perhaps down near to you, might have a son who likes to torment the neighbors for reasons only he is aware. Sometimes he steals petty things, hides their trash barrels, places one family's decorative statue in another family's yard: things of that sort. This began at least five years ago." I said I was sorry to hear this. But it was before we had learned anything about the Macintoshes or the students next door to us and I was thinking this "kid" was probably part of history by now. I soon forgot about the conversation.

Now Mrs. Bancroft's words hauntingly came back to me although again I quickly dismissed them as the Trooper had just assured us this young man was living far away. At least all his behaviors seemed relatively benign with, in my opinion, the exceptions of the egging and the rat, whoever the culprit is. The rat ended up involving the authorities and truly upsetting Terry and the egging had been a huge aggravation and cost us sleep. If Joseph Macintosh was still harassing neighbors then I saw his activities as escalating and he was operating despite the law wishing to work with him. In my mind he was a fugitive from justice.

24

CHRISTMAS IN OUR NEW HOME

I have always been crazy about Christmas, perhaps because it often brought my then divided family closer together or because some years I was celebrating in two countries; but in any case it was busy and joyful. Now, in the first home of our own I was nearly manic with the need to celebrate in grand style.

We had six working fireplaces and that meant six mantels. Each mantel had green garlands hanging from it and was decorated as the Victorians might have done with angels and gorgeous Saint Nicholases, candles and fancy china pieces. There was a cornucopia on the dining room table and it was stuffed with beautiful fruit; fresh but green pears, candied fruit and a few exquisitely crafted works of hand blown glass fruit. There were little tiny mice sitting around a tiny Christmas tree in my China cupboard looking as though they too were celebrating.

In a corner of the second parlor I had an antique doll house which Matt had purchased for me on our first anniversary. By this time I had crafted, purchased at special sales or mail ordered fabulous tiny reproduction furniture for each room. I even had special decorations for four seasons with Christmas being the most lavish. And at Christmas we plugged it in to enjoy its electricity. It held a ceramic, lit Christmas tree!

Our primary Christmas tree was in the main parlor in a window across from the fireplace. It was not huge as these rooms had the original low ceilings designed to make heating more efficient. The tree was not as glittery as the one we put in the second parlor near the doll house. This tree was less Victorian in orientation and more Early American. There were candles (which we would never light due to the hazard of open flames on drying trees), natural and spray painted pine cones, little groupings of acorns that had been sprayed gold and large lace-like ribbons tied on many branches. A handmade sleigh that my American grandfather had built sat under the tree holding a cloth baby doll crafted by my grandmother.

There were actually Christmas trees in all rooms save the bathrooms. Each tree had a distinct theme so in addition to Early American and Victorian there was country rustic, a whimsical cooking theme on the kitchen tree, stars, angels, Santas, jungle animals, Christmas candy and dogs. It sounds exhausting but it was fun for me and I owned many of these miniature collections from my travels. My mother arrived a few days before Christmas and together we decorated, cooked and wrapped. We had invited a few friends, both old and new, in for a Christmas Eve open house. That and the recent arrival of Scruffy made this a very exciting time plus we were toasting Matt's tenure. The letter had arrived from the Provost with the proviso that it would be endorsed at the March meeting of the Board of Trustees.

This gave us an opportunity to invite Terry and his fiancé to the party as a peace offering. Matt and I wanted no hard feelings and a celebration, with the Dean in attendance, would make the relationship more comfortable for Terry and Matt. We also invited the students from next door, Priscilla, Adam and of course Fred and many of the workmen who had done so much for us in a fairly short time frame. Peter, of Pest Service fame, was the only one who declined the invitation. Peter could well have had personal commitments on Christmas Eve but Matt and I both sensed that perhaps he wished to avoid the scene of his horrible experience with the spiders even though we had assured him that the extermination process had worked well, well pretty well.

Matt set up a bar in the second parlor to force traffic through the house as two doors led into the kitchen. We figured if most people entered through the kitchen there was a high probability that they would not leave that room. Since this was intended as an open house and every room was decorated we truly wanted circulation throughout. Of course the dining room was directly off the kitchen so serving food would only get them to move a few feet. My mother suggested placing hors d' oeuvres on trays throughout the house and even putting desserts upstairs and announcing that to the guests. It worked like a charm as most of our friends seemed to prefer eating desserts before the main courses were served!

We had mixed music playing which included some Christmas carols but for many reasons we did not wish to make the theme tiresome especially for non-Christian friends. My father, who had by now joined us, kidded me that all those trees would be tiresome enough for those who didn't much care for Christmas. I countered with our hope that the food would compensate those guests. We had antipasto, melon and prosciutto, several different lasagna's – some with seafood, some with vegetables and several with meat, meatballs, shrimp, cold salmon and gnocchi with pesto. Matt said he was looking forward to the leftovers as we had often been too busy to do much cooking.

Christmas in the new home passed as an old fashioned and joyous occasion. My mother had not celebrated many Christmases in the United States and thought it was one holiday we Americans did better than the Italians. She loved all the trimming, glitter, gifts and snow. Our antique home certainly was at its coziest with a coating of snow on the ground and fires crackling in two or more fireplaces. Two days after Christmas we were sad to see my parents leave but they had lives to return to and we actually had a New Year's Eve party to attend at the home of one of Matt's colleagues who also lived fairly close to the campus. Finally our drama appeared to be dying down and our home was lovely to enter rather than a disaster with workmen, wallpaper and dust as the primary focus.

25

ENTER 2020

The New Year's Eve Party was a bit reserved. Our host couple was both extremely scholarly and hadn't really dressed up for the night as was our custom. They each wore tweed pants and warm sweaters as opposed to me in a long black dress with rhinestones sewn into the bodice and Matt in a tuxedo; but we weren't alone in our city style. Several other folks were dressed as much as I and Matt wasn't the only black tie. Well, we would ask more questions another time should we be invited back. Alternatively perhaps we needed to acclimate to this relaxed country style.

The house was impressive in the number of books it contained. Thirty years our seniors these people must never have thrown a book out and thought nothing of making a room smaller by using every square inch of wall space as bookshelves. In front of many books were objects d' art and on the outer cross pieces of shelving several paintings were hanging by nails. There was just enough space behind each work of art so that you might, very carefully, remove a book. Even the backs of doors, where possible, were bookshelves and the staircase was edged with a brimming bookcase so that one might halt part way up and sit down on the stairs for a good read.

There was a charm to this and yet it was so cramped and overstuffed that I began to have trouble breathing; perhaps I am a closet claustrophobic – pun intended. In any case one way they saved on space was to offer a very light meal. We had been told there would be plenty of food, not to bring anything as they loved to cook, but we soon realized that the hors d' oeuvres were, in fact, dinner. Not Italians. What can you do? So while we were trying to restrain our appetites thus leaving enough sustenance for others, our hosts began to look at the clock and announced that they wished us all a Happy New Year but they intended to end their party by 10 PM with our safety and good health in mind.

Initially I thought it was a joke. In Italy this is when the party usually began but no; others were getting their coats so we too followed the pack. Once in the car I asked Matt what had just happened and then we started to laugh. "One of life's experiences," he chuckled. Then "shall we look for someplace to go dancing or head home?" I almost said "the night is young" but then I thought of how happy Scruffy and Sybil would be to see us so I suggested we go home. It was the best decision I might ever have made.

As we started up our driveway I saw a strange orange glow in the main parlor and without really knowing what I was saying I shouted "Matt, fire!" Then I dialed 911 and he and I rushed into the house. I got the animals out and forced them into our car shutting the door behind them. Matt took a beautiful oriental rug, the first thing he could find, and threw it over the Christmas tree which was by now totally engulfed in flames. He smothered the fire while I used a just purchased fire extinguisher on the edges of curtains and an ottoman that had been too close to the tree. By the time the volunteer fire fighters arrived we were opening all windows and doors to let the smoke out.

I was near tears to think about redoing so much in the "prettiest" room in our house but I was also incredulous at our good luck to have been kicked out of a New Year's Eve party before midnight! The firefighters looked everything over to be certain we wouldn't be victims of a flare up while we slept but they determined we were clear. Several times the firefighters remarked as to how lucky we were to have saved the place. All of us asked "but how did this get started". I answered that the tree had held real candles but they were simply decorative and had never been lit nor had we ever intended them to be. Also, in response to the firefighter's query about a possible electrical shortage, I explained this tree had not been strung with any lights; it was strictly an Early American theme. The more we attempted to determine the fire's cause the more anxious I became suspecting that once again we had been the victims of a prank but this time the prank was definitely not humorous nor harmless. This time we really needed help from the State Troopers. We had almost lost a 250 year old house which we had just completely renovated, our computers and all our worldly goods and our dear dog and cat!

As the firefighters turned to leave one of them noted it had just become 2020 and wished us a Happy New Year! We thanked them very much for spending their celebration with us and said we expected that at least 2020 would be luckier than 2019 had been. They agreed saying the repairs we needed were minimal and we should easily be able to sleep in the house with no additional airing. And so Matt and I, with concerns for what might happen next, went to get our pets and settle in for the night.

By morning, with very little sleep, we were up and on the phone with the local barracks of the State Police despite the fact that it was

New Year's Day. They wanted to send a "detective" over to investigate the scene. When Sergeant Parker arrived it was 10:30 AM and, of course, the fire had been out for nearly 12 hours. We had also had permission from the firefighters to clean up the mess. Apparently this was of little consequence to the detective as she wanted to go over our history of problems. We related the strange delivery to the backdoor of our dead cat, the stolen beach chair, the near death of our exterminator, the moaning and open doors in the middle of the night, the repeated egging of the house also during the middle of the night and the receipt, via the US Postal Service, of one dead rat. The coup de gras was last night with the attempted arson of our home. I noted there actually was arson as the tree had been incinerated and some furniture and a rug damaged.

Sergeant Parker was a very serious woman probably about forty years old, tall in stature and a no nonsense African American woman who generated confidence that this time the job would be handled thoroughly. She noted everything on an official form, asked us each to initial it and then signed her name. She reviewed the miniscule list of suspects with us, the only one of whom now lived in Kentucky, and said she would check on a few things including making contact with both the Macintoshes and this youngest son. She thought it was time to ascertain exactly where he was living on this precise date.

Then she asked for permission to walk out back just to take her own look at the former encampment. Certainly we said and Matt offered to accompany her which she politely but crisply refused. However she did suggest our dog would make a good escort so she entered the woods with Scruffy on a leash and a pocket full of dog treats. It made the dog very happy and showed her human side.

Later when Sergeant Parker returned from the back acres she seemed pleased about something but wouldn't say what. She thanked us for the loan of Scruffy and returned a very happy dog full of wiggles in gratitude for the attention she had given him. She promised to work on this case and to get back to us fairly quickly. In the meantime she advised that we remain on high alert, let the dog patrol the yard as much as possible, and not to take anything for granted. Apparently there is a typical pattern among some perpetrators where they will continue to escalate their attacks until they have done real damage to the objects of their anger. The reason we were said objects was simply by virtue of buying the house next door to his childhood home and a property from which that homestead had been cut. That is, assuming the culprit was indeed young Macintosh.

We spent another restless night. Scruffy, who is crate trained and therefore sleeps happily in a little confined area each night, was left loose in the house. We wanted him to have access to any area of the place that might draw his attention while we were asleep. Of course he had not lived in this house long and found all facets of the old place fascinating. He was up wandering around as soon as we were no longer paying attention to him.

Initially, while I lay in bed, I tried to follow the sounds of his travels. It was difficult as he went up and down the stairs and would then turn in several circles near our bed before settling down. The hope was he would fall asleep but awaken easily if his nose and ears received any triggers at all. But if the perpetrator was watching the house he would already be aware that we were home, that we had a dog with us and that the State Police were more than just casually interested in him.

What eventually roused us awake in the morning was not Scruffy, who appeared to be sleeping in, but the telephone to the house. Sergeant Parker called to say she had definite news and was heading over. The Macintoshes disavowed any knowledge of where their son was for the last five days but he certainly was not staying with them. They had seen him briefly, celebrated Christmas and then he took off. They had no idea what State he was in. They cautioned the Officer that they thought he was "off his medicine again and they had no way of forcing him to be compliant." "Oh goody" was the only response I could muster.

Sergeant Parker said there would be an alert out to find this man especially here in Connecticut. Further they would have an unmarked car drive by our home every two hours. Finally she suggested that we not leave our home unattended, that is, if Matt had to be somewhere then it would be best for me to remain in the house and vice versa; just until they find this guy she added.

Matt wanted to know if we should be armed. The Sergeant didn't believe that would help but left us each a can of Mace and gave us directions for use in case of an emergency. Her belief was that he would not show up armed and why give him a weapon at ready disposal by caring guns since we don't know how his mind works. Then she added that there had been a little personal mail hidden under some leaves in a plastic bag that Scruffy had helped her discover when they went on their walk the previous day. One of the return addresses was for a long time classmate of this Joe Macintosh and the State Police were keeping an eye on his place, also in East Apple, to see if Joe turned up there.

Once the Officer left, Matt asked if I minded him running into campus to check on his University mailbox; I said no, I felt safe, after all I had Scruffy. And I thought, with Christmas over and most of the decorations down, I could now turn my attention to Emily's notes that I found weeks ago in the old barn.

26

EMILY'S LIFE CONTINUES

And so with Matt at the University I took out the last words I was aware of that had been written by Emily Harrison Wilbur.

I don't know exactly when I stopped writing. I think it was shortly after Will told me that he could not come back to me. I remember that Ben's wife died shortly after that and Ben proposed to me and life just seemed to whirl in a vortex trapping me. I had spent over forty years being prim and proper, taking care to help my parents and my brothers when they were around. Volunteering at the Church was a big step for me as it put me out of the house every day but I didn't take that on until my folks were gone. What worked to my advantage was that I liked arithmetic and grammar and had studied them enough to get ahead of most people so I had skills that actually helped the Church. I could correspond and keep track of the books just about better than any of them. I'd done the books for my folks' farm and handled their estate so I knew my way around a few things and I knew a lawyer or two plus the bankers nearby.

Ben surprised me by saying we should marry as I had never dared entertain such a notion especially as he was married already and I was so much older. Still, it tickled me to think he meant it. And with time he continued to propose so I started to take him seriously. The proposals did help to distract me from my grief over Will and Ben's youngest daughters were most kind to me. Ginny, the eldest was in Boston most of the time but we traveled there once for her wedding. It was a beautiful affair in the biggest Church I had ever seen near a picturesque and busy harbor. Such excitement!

Anyway, I made Ben wait for our marriage for over a year. I didn't want anyone, like that spiteful old Mrs. Alabaster, to discredit Ben for marrying too soon after he had lost his wife. And so things were timed such that he retired as Pastor of the Church and I retired as Secretary just before the nuptials. Ben's retirement meant that he could no longer live in the parsonage which was fine by me as I preferred my own home and didn't want to be sleeping on the late-wife's side of the bed. We had the wedding the very next day before anyone needed to move in at his house and as I wanted us to start off fresh in my home.

As a girl I had dreamt about my wedding, I think most girls do, but by twenty when I had no prospects I had pretty much wiped those ideas from my mind. So to be marrying in my mid-fifties was a mixture of joy and embarrassment. Also, a number of the Church ladies who were widows or who had widowed sisters had been very excited about the prospect of snagging the Reverend as a husband. He had been the recipient of all manner of casseroles, cakes and smoked hams the moment his poor wife stopped breathing.

Due to my age and appearance none of these ladies must have seen me as a contender for his hand. Several of them actually queried me about Ben as though I should conspire with them to foster their cause! Did I think he liked cream pies, or did he seem to favor women in bonnets, or was the fact he was educated likely to be a barrier if they were not well read? I nearly choked each time they confided in me but I simply said the truth, thus far the Reverend had not shown any interest in pursuing women. Not mentioning, of course, because he already had me.

So we elected not to invite the entire Church to our wedding. We thought it, as he was a widower, unseemly to make too much of an occasion of this event; I wanted to modestly and without much fanfare, pass from Miss to Mrs. The girls helped me make a cream colored dress that could easily be used for curtains once the day was over. We all did a little baking and the roses in my yard cooperated so that the place really decorated itself. I carried a bouquet of pink hydrangeas, also from the yard, and the buffet table held a similar vase of flowers. That day I actually felt pretty.

All three of Ben's daughters were there with their spouses or fiancés and Ben's best friend from the Seminary came down from Boston to perform our service. One of my brothers traveled considerable distance to join us although the trip was too exhausting for his family to have accompanied him. I think he just wanted to see with his own eyes that someone had finally married his sister. I imagine Ben's still youthful good looks gave him quite a surprise. And so on November 21, 1823 I became Mrs. Benjamin Wilbur at age 55. It was a delightful day for me in all ways but one.

If our dear son could have celebrated this occasion with us life would have been perfect. I thought about him resting only a few feet below us and wondered what he could feel or sense. Did he know we were near him and planned to spend the rest of our days with him? Or did he have a dreamless sleep? When a few spiders, small and not related to Annabella, showed themselves at the buffet I would not let anyone shoo them away; just in case, I thought, just in case they are bringing messages to my boy.

But after the wedding, and our little celebration had transpired, Ben wanted us to lead a simple life without he said "always looking in the cellar for a ghost." He loved to speak of Will and Will's clever ways but he all but forbade me to try and conjure up some sign from Will; and we were both none too keen on spiders. So I did as my husband suggested and did all I could to live a "normal" life. Ben continued to provide me with love and consideration and also worked by my side.

We planted and harvested the crops together; he butchered the meat while I did the canning and, as I was older, he was considerate of assisting with cleaning especially the heavier duties. He brought in the firewood and most of the buckets of water. On Sundays we would have a day of rest typically taking a gentle walk to the church where we politely listened to the new preacher. This man wasn't an ordained minister like Ben but very talented and he looked up to Ben. I daresay Ben got to enjoy some fatherly feelings by mentoring Pastor Grady.

And Ben wanted to travel! No, we didn't go away on a ship but I had hardly been out of East Apple so Ben's taking us to Boston, New York and the beautiful coast of Rhode Island were a thrill for me. I saw sights and met people that gave my old heart joy and I learned to enjoy more seafood. It was just that every now and again I wanted to share some artifact with Will or bring him a little shell for his collection but I did not feel that such a notion could even be mentioned.

When you own a farm, especially with farm animals, your travels must be limited. We imposed on Levy and Esther often enough to fill in for us and they had their own families to consider. Naturally we were very generous with them whenever they needed the least little thing. It was our intention to pass my farm along to those two, who had remained close-by, when the time came to bury us. It often felt as though I did have grown daughters and their children meant the world to me.

The question of burial was a difficult one. For some unknown reason I simply did not seem to age very fast. I had slowed some and had my aches and pains but my hair had hardly grayed, my eyesight was still sharp and my hearing quite acute. However in Ben the pace of time was marked. Perhaps all that wood chopping had ruined his back after a fashion. And, although his mind was good, his eyesight and hearing were bad enough that I had to read to him in a loud voice so he could keep up with family news from Ginny. It was a sign to me that he might pass on first even though I was considerably his elder.

Thus I felt compelled to determine his wishes for burial should the decision fall to me. I knew he and the first Mrs. Wilbur had originally planned to be buried together up the hill. When she had passed on we had brought Will's gravestone here to my farm where we placed it behind the barn. No one had asked why Will's name was not included on the family plot she was now in.

In any case there was enough room remaining in that plot for his daughters and their families; and, as far as the world knew, "our adopted son" was indeed buried there although certainly a few folks had other knowledge. I began encouraging Ben to speak to Pastor Grady about his burial and service.

Ben was concerned that I should not, after all the love and time I was giving him, feel displaced from being at his side for eternity. I advised him that if I felt that way and he went first I would simply join him but face away from his first wife. And so Ben was comforted near the end of his days believing that I would remain at his side. I thought about that, I truly did, but what I really wanted was a way to end up in the ground next to Will. I needed a plan or a discrete confidant to enable me to be buried the way that I chose. I also wasn't certain what subterfuge might be required so that I wouldn't be plunked in the ground up the hill. Toward that end I started grooming one of Levy's children.

The boy I chose was strong enough so that in a few years he could both drag me along and dig a deep hole. He was poised enough to keep matters to himself if there was a good reason; and I thought him remarkably adult-like and stable. I did not want to drive a young man crazy with my request so he would need a serene and mature outlook. I was also prepared to back off this plan at the slightest sign that I was creating a problem for him.

I began by showing him Will's portrait and telling him how I came to be Will's "mother." I painted a most positive picture of Will and his love of critters, his collections and ambition. In fact, while his grandfather was still relatively agile, we went through Will's collection of shells, skulls and skeletons to see what might be interesting for young Theodor.

Ben knew I never wanted to part with Will's collection but he had observed my closeness to this boy and thought it would be healthy for me to give up a few of those reminders of Will. We also agreed that Theodor would find these items fascinating especially if we presented them in the right manner: with the joy and curiosity that they had engendered in Will.

As hoped, Teddy, found the items most curious. He marveled at the skeletons and exoskeletal remains Will had saved. He read several of Will's books and stared at his drawings. He even began to trace one of the starfish and then to shade it in with charcoals. Then he found the book on "Exotic Nature of the Amazon" and immediately became excited by the description of the Goliath Bird Eater.

Ben sensed my immediate discomfort and said to our grandson "That's probably enough book work for one day. Why don't you bring me my walking stick and we'll go out back for a look at nature in vivo." "In vivo?" Teddy replied, "Yes, in life" said Ben. "There is plenty to see in your own back fields although some of the more interesting things may be under a rock or a log or on the edge of the pond. Bring a jar with a lid and let's go." It sounded very much as it had years before when he was first lighting the flame of curiosity under Will. I smiled as I put the book back on the shelf.

This was the start of many happy adventures among the three of us and particularly Teddy and Ben. We were always certain to extend an open invitation to all the grandchildren who might wish to go "exploring" with us in the backyard once chores were done or after church on Sundays but Teddy always came and nearly always alone. Our feelings were not hurt. We knew the other kids had precious little free time as all were expected to perform significant chores at home and several continued with school work. But Teddy automatically made us a priority and we grew to believe he sincerely enjoyed working with and learning from us.

We really were starting to slow down. Ben could simply not physically manage the farm duties and I could not step in as a substitute on matters which required tossing a bale of hay, lugging bags of feed or distributing pails of water. I could pick our crops, harvest the eggs and pickle anything but the heavy butchering would need to be done by someone else. Ben would try and keep up with lightweight repairs, and could still swing a hammer pretty well, but he could not do this for long and not without a few unpastor-like words escaping from his lips. I hasten to add that he was never before a man prone to profanity, in fact he loathed crudeness, but he was tired and his body wearing out.

And so it became obvious, first to us and then to Teddy and finally to the family, that we needed more than a little help; with permission from Levy and her husband we invited Teddy to live with us and work the hours he could but still go to school. We had many bedrooms and he chose a simple one with two windows. The door to the attic was through his room so this gave him an opportunity to explore in the evenings. The attic held more of Will's materials on the collection. It was also the destination of his grandfather's sermons when we had needed a place for these files to be stored and there were actually still papers up there from my parents and from the Judge who had built our house. No one ever fully cleaned out an attic!

We slipped into a companionable routine: I would rise early as did Teddy. While he milked the few cows and distributed feed I would cook eggs and ham, pour glasses of milk and cut a slice of last night's pie. We would leave a plate for Ben who would usually join us although a bit later. Then I would make a sack lunch for Ted and he would head to school. Once he was gone I'd help Ben to get washed and dressed for the day and seat him on the porch where he could keep an eye on things. He generally liked to have a book by his side. When he was comfortable I would harvest the eggs, fruit and vegetables which were ready and often cut and begin drying the herbs. If someone came by to purchase apples or other products Ben would see that they were accommodated. And thus we continued for several years which were highlighted by the Christian holidays and family get-togethers; with Teddy's help we also still managed to get to church nearly every week.

It wasn't long after Christmas of 1855 that Ben tripped or slipped in the barnyard, falling and breaking his hip. He remained coherent and optimistic for several days before lapsing into a coma and then succumbing to pneumonia. While he lingered, both Levy and Esther helped me with his care. Of course the doctor had been summoned but there was nothing to be done for him except help to ease the pain prior to the coma, with an elixir that seemed also to make poor Ben too sleepy to speak. I reasoned at this point he needed the sleep more than talking, we had been very close and discussed everything, well, almost everything, for the thirty three years of our marriage and the twelve prior years when we had Will. I had been his wife longer than his first wife and took a certain private pride in that. While this was going on Teddy would look in on his grandfather for a few minutes each day and then resume his duties with increased vigor as though proving to himself that he could handle the place.

When it was time to let Ben go to his Heavenly Father I shed many a tear but did not feel the world had come to an end. Joyously for him he had remained conscious long enough to have one last conversation with Ginny, when she and her family arrived from Boston, his other girls and Teddy. We had a lovely reception in the house to honor him. The church, in gratitude for his years as Pastor, gave him a beautiful service and hung a plaque to honor him. He was then buried up the hill next to his late wife in their family plot. Notably there was space remaining for those of us coming to the grave after him.

A short time later the girls sat down with me and decided that Esther, her husband and three of their four girls would move into my house with me. Their oldest daughter and her husband had already been living with them on a rather small dairy farm. They would now turn over that farm to the young couple while the rest of the family helped me to carry on the work Ben and I had been doing here.

A most agreeable arrangement; at a later date they thought to sell off parcels of the land to allow Levy's three boys a share each. It was necessary for me to declare that Teddy had been a major help to us for years and that his grandfather and I wished to have him inherit certain educational materials, and our team of wagon horses as well as his share of the land. Esther had been aware that he worked for us and agreed that this sounded equitable.

Of course this pleasant arrangement left me with a bit of a predicament; how was Teddy going to manage the secret plan I had, should my death occur when I was surrounded by this dear family of Esther's? Who would be preparing me for my trip to eternity anyway and how could I slip away from the coffin traveling up the hill when I wanted to be in the cellar dirt: unless I seemed to disappear never to be *seen again or ran away presumably in a demented state and was never recovered? It was one matter for Ben and I to stuff Will's coffin thus keeping him home but quite another to make this switch when I, in fact, would no longer be living.*

Well, the good news was that I was feeling quite well so perhaps I had a few years to ponder this dilemma. After all, there is a solution to everything, even needing a little life after death. Or maybe I needed to begin practicing my role as a forgetful person to augment my needing to convince them at the end that I was senile, and just have Teddy at the ready when it was time to disappear for good - or one hundred years or so.

27

THE DISAPPEARANCE OF EMILY HARRISON WILBUR

As Matt had not yet returned from his laboratory I continued to read with only a glance around the yard for any sign of Joe. Scruffy lay calmly beside me.

It was more of an adjustment having Esther, and most of her family, move in than I had reckoned on. She was still very dear to me but Ben and I had relished our privacy and Teddy had so quietly fit in that it seemed the house was now always in an uproar. Still, although work was added, her husband was an ambitious helper and the three girls who lived here were good bakers so I simply had to just let them take over. I didn't have to wash a sheet or stir the lye into the soap or fetch the eggs as Esther was up before me. Even Teddy seemed glad of their help and complimented them on the meals while being careful to be considerate of me. But as each day passed I again pondered how would I manage to be dead in two places at the same time?

It must have troubled my mind considerably for when I awoke in the morning I found the closet door wide open and the trap door slung back to permit someone to go down to the cellar or to come up. I must have walked in my sleep. I had no memory of doing this but the evidence was clear. I quickly and quietly placed things as they should be and went downstairs to find fresh blueberry muffins. I simply acted as though nothing had happened but to test my supposition I inquired if anyone had heard anything in the night? One of the girls said she had gone out to the outhouse early but didn't think she had made any particular noise. I reassured her that my question meant nothing significant and I might have had a bad dream. We moved on to other things.

But that night my spirit was again restless and this time I had a more detailed recall of a dream. I awoke from a deep sleep and descended the stairs to the cellar. Something then drew me outside via the bulkhead. In the dream Teddy was waiting for me and said "Ben would like us to explore for interesting insects. He has advised us to go to the barn but be careful where we step." So without another word I followed him to the barn where we began scraping around side boards and lifting materials which had been stored in corners. Soon a pair of hairy legs appeared from below the barn and began to propel a creature of considerable size up from the depths. It shook itself off and I recognized it to be Annabella!

I screamed and fainted and then later woke up in my own bed, presumably carried there by Teddy. But I did arise to a normal looking room, no closet door ajar and roughly at my usual time for breakfast. My heart was racing but I placed my hand on my chest and tried to relax knowing this had all been a dream. A couple of deep breathes and I reached out for my slippers — which were caked in mud.

I sat heavily back down on the bed. What had happened last night? Then I realized that I could well have been dreaming and sleep walking which would explain the mud on my slippers; that dirt was not proof that I had been in the barn and actually seen Annabella or her kin. An enormous wave of relief started at the top of my head and went to the tips of my toes. I could not handle the shock and horror of that nightmare. But I was safe at home in my own bed after all.

I went downstairs to breakfast feeling just a little wobbly. Esther greeted me with "Well you are a sleepy head today" but said nothing more sinister than that. Then she added, "Teddy is out in the barn and asked if you would join him when you have a chance." "Oh," I countered, "did he indicate what he wanted?"

She replied "No, I just think it is one of those nature things you and grandpa were always chasing after with him, some wonder of nature on the farm" she ended with almost a laugh.

I hurried my meal along as the coincidence of his request in proximity to last night's dream did cause me some unrest. I soon found Teddy putting down some floor boards that must have been a bit warped due to a small leak in the barn roof. I must have come up behind him too quietly for he jumped a foot high when I first spoke. I apologized for giving him a fright and then asked what he had wanted to see me about.

"Well, Grammy," he began "you probably don't remember but you were walking in your sleep again last night. I found you out here passed out cold when your scream awoke me. I was just trying to see what all the fuss was about."

I replied, "Well thank you very much Teddy for coming to my rescue. I had no idea how my slippers got so dirty unless I had been walking around again. So you had to carry me back in?"

"Yes ma'am. Are you okay and what do you recall?"

It was then that I took Teddy into my confidence, speaking of my need to be buried secretly with my son Will, in our very cellar. I mentioned now that Grandpa was gone only one other person knew Will was down there and he'd never talk, so I needed Teddy to become my confidential ally. I ended with the request that upon my death he place me into the ground with Will and be certain no one else was aware of my final destination. I also cautioned him that no matter what he encountered as he dug into the cellar floor, he was not to become frightened or to react. And under no circumstance was he to remove anything he unearthed. Whatever bones or critters there might be were to be reinterred with me no matter how vile he might find them; and then he must push this all out of his mind and not ruminate on any of it.

Teddy looked shocked but finally said, "If that is what you want I will do it for you but I don't know how to keep others from noticing your body is missing."

"Well, Teddy, I have a plan but it will be tricky. First I am going to have to pretend to become increasingly forgetful so that wandering off will seem ordinary behavior for me. Now as a God-fearing Christian woman I cannot take my own life but when I know the time to go join your grandfather and Will is near I will walk or crawl away. It may even happen that I will need you to take me into the woods and just set me down to rest for awhile. When you return, God willing, I will be gone and you can place my shell, for that is all the body is, into the cellar ground."

To my surprise Teddy was crying. His jaw trembling he said, "I don't want you to die."

I replied, "Thank you dear boy, but all of us come to that end eventually and I have no possibility of lasting much longer. Truth be known I am now near 100 years old as I was considerably older than your grandfather. I had best start my 'acting' soon. I also have a beautiful ring to give you. It had belonged to my mother and I want you to have it for all the help you are to me. None of the others have even seen it so you just sell it when you wish or give it to some lucky lady in the future but it should help with your start in life."

The next day I passed a gold ring with two diamonds in it into Teddy's hand and asked him to take me back to Esther saying he found me wandering in the field. I also explained that I wouldn't be asking him to tell stories very often as I knew I'd be a bad influence. He laughed at this.

Within two months I was obviously slipping both due to my pretend forgetfulness and my actual loss of weight due to poor health. Tomorrow I plan to have Teddy take me out back late in the day and leave me until night fall. I pray I can hang on that long. The End, Emily H. Wilbur, September 28, 1869.

28

DAWNING OF THE DARK

And Emily's Diary ended here. Of course she could give no indication if Teddy was able to help her carry out her plan and to what extent it was successful. Perhaps the family looked for her for a long time, perhaps someone interrupted Teddy on his mission, perhaps he broke down and confessed all; the final details have faded away with Teddy's passing. Just as at the end of any good story I knew I would miss her.

I reminded myself that if the diaries were factual then there are two human bodies buried in our cellar. And one of these human remains passed on believing that the spider bites which killed him would also resurrect him after a significant period of dormancy. Could there be any truth to this? I know cicadas lay dormant underground for up to seventeen years, and anthrax spores keep their potency for many years but to arise from the grave after something like two hundred years defies credulity whether we are discussing a man or an arachnid. Still I continued to be disconcerted to think two sets of bones are down in the basement. At the very least we may wish to have them moved to the graveyard up the hill where they were originally intended to be. I'm sure we could reinter them with respect and dignity. Matt and I will discuss this again tonight.

Just as I finished reading all of this I was jolted back to the present. Matt and I were on shifts guarding the house from Joe Macintosh who seemed determined to cause us harm. Then Matt returned from the University and he was in a fairly upbeat mood. He told me there had been several notes of congratulations on his Tenure having been granted and he felt most of his anxiety dissipate regarding the future. The office had been quiet due to the holiday allowing him not only to collect his thoughts but to enjoy a moment of joy until he thought about a mentally ill ex-neighbor lurking about our home. He told me when this possibility entered his mind he had grabbed his laptop and made the drive home.

I guess Matt was surprised because I wasn't trembling with fear over an imminent attack by Joe Macintosh; but I was fairly concerned over the last part of the old diary I had been reading. Matt allowed me to read the final entries to him as written in the 1860's by a woman I told him was named Emily. Further, I told Matt that I was more convinced than ever that Emily and her son were buried in the basement along with some of those spiders we thought we had eradicated and that spiders, mother and son, would soon appear too from that humble resting place.

"Unless this was superstitious nonsense," Matt uttered. Matt didn't seem to care if he offended me. He added, "You have a scientific background, and you are well read, have you ever heard of any experience where such an occurrence has happened?"

I explained about the cicadas and the logical tone of the diary. I at least wanted Matt to consider that the bodies were buried in the dirt floor of our house. He said he could acknowledge that as a possibility. So then I suggested we explore this, not as a concept but with a pick and shovel. Matt again promised that as soon as it warmed up a bit more outside it might be easier to have a look inside. This kept me quiet for the moment.

Now we were readying for bed. Matt booby trapped the two most logical doors for an intruder to use, those with entry from the woods. Scruffy was petted and seemed only too happy to have free run of the house again as we went upstairs to bed leaving him on duty at the ground level. We shut off the lights and settled in for what we hoped would be a good night's sleep on a cold January night in New England. Surprisingly after so much excitement we were both very tired and fell into deep sleeps knowing we were as prepared as possible.

But little did we know that the best laid plans were about to implode. Joe Macintosh had already been laying in wait within our house. He was crouched in a corner of a spare bedroom upstairs and the fact that I had not as yet found places to store everything provided great cover for him. Apparently he had made friends with Scruffy days ago and although the dear dog could detect his presence, Scruffy never thought to react as it was just another friend about the place. And tonight the "friend" thought first to feed Scruffy ham laced with a strong tranquilizer, just as he had dissolved into our water pitcher. We took the nice cold pitcher upstairs as we always do at night. We didn't realize that everyone, except Sybil, was now drugged.

Once we were nearly unconscious Joe hastened to carry out his devious plans. Apparently he first tied Matt and bound him to the headboard with handcuffs. The drug was just strong enough to prevent Matt from waking. Matt simply incorporated the few sensations into the dream he was experiencing. Then Joe repeated this with me whom he truly disliked as he saw me as having been poking into his life and causing him trouble with the police. He thought about doing terrible things to me but that would come later. Then he went through our personal items seeking anything of value and wishing to find the deed to our home. Somehow I could not move but my senses were alert to the fact he was here. Maybe I was part witch after all. I could hear him opening and closing drawers in a rough and angry manner.

He became frustrated as he could only discover a few trinkets and no legal papers. He switched strategies and decided it would be best to have us awake so that he could question us and enjoy our fear. How dare we claim ownership to this place and this land he would later mutter to us? He had always played here, explored here, fantasized here and had seen himself as owner, farmer, and future hub of the community using the bounty of the land to feed local needs and as a basis for several businesses. His parents hadn't wanted to invest in him but this house and land were going down in value while it lay empty for many years. He could have bought it with just a little help; he would rant at us, until I came along with my enthusiasm and grand ideas. I had even had the nerve to call the police while he was living in his simple camp in the back. What was my problem he wondered? He was doing no harm and no one else was ever out there except during hunting season when he would go away. After all, he recalled, his kin had owned this land.

He couldn't wait to see me face to face; he relished the notion of my terror. "Let's see how clever and resilient you are when you meet the true owner of this farm!" Joe muttered. With those words Joe unlocked my cuffs from the bed and relocked them in front of me so that he could drag or pull me along. To his joy I appeared quite dazed and was compliant with everything he asked. Soon he had me retied to a chair in the kitchen where he left me while going back for Matt. I wanted to continue to be quiet as I wished to have him underestimate me. I know he was anticipating the torment on Matt's face when he began to torture me. "You will soon know how I've felt every time you've changed a door or a window or added a porch or beam; you don't have the right to do this, it is my property!" Joe shrieked at us.

Matt was more difficult to deal with. Not only was he heavier but the tranquilizer appeared to be wearing off him faster than I allowed it to show on me. Matt became restless when Joe began moving him around and then he became belligerent flailing his arms out as though trying to strike Joe from many angles. Joe finally punched the side of poor Matt's head and that slowed him down long enough for them to get down the stairs where Joe then bound him to the chair with both cuffs and a rope. Although perspiring and cursing, Joe was also laughing a mean sounding chortle as he worked. Joe said, "It felt so good to finally hit you, doctor."

When he had us both properly tied to the kitchen seats he decided he'd better have another look at Scruffy. The dog was having labored breathing which made Joe question the dose of medication he had given him. It was intended for humans so Joe reasoned it wasn't his fault if he had given the poor critter too much. But I guess he liked dogs, so instead of risking killing him, he rolled him onto a small rug and tugged him over to the cellar stairs where he gently pushed him down and locked the door behind him. "No need having this dog turn into a hero when I'm playing rough with his mistress," Joe muttered.

And then he began his party. First he threw a pitcher of ice water at each of us shocking us into wakefulness and forcing us to come out of our stupors feeling as though we were drowning, gasping and coughing violently. Then he addressed each of us by name and introduced himself as the "Owner of the Back Acres". He explained that we were causing him trouble and he was there to take over our deed and he would teach us what it felt like to be ignored and treated as a degenerate. He also said he hadn't been with a woman since rehab many years ago and he thought I owed him a good time. If we did as we were told, and signed over the deed, we would be let go once he felt we had repented enough.

Instantly I thought: So here is our boogie man; this is the face of the person who lurks in houses during the night, who lives out back in the woods and steals any petty thing he needs; who impersonates a ghost and who has tried to burn this house down when he couldn't intimidate us enough to make us run away. This is the man whose own family was so disenchanted with him that they chose to move away rather than to deal with him! I was repulsed and felt sick to my stomach. He was bearded and filthy and his features were distorted in a maniacal grin while he spewed vindictives.

Matt, always the astute psychologist began to speak first, "Look Joe, we never intended to take what was yours" he apologized. "We were using a realtor who had presented this property as available and the current owners had even been anxious to sell. We had thought we were acting in good faith and had paid a fair price." Matt ended by saying "We just wanted what was best for the history of the house and for the appearance of the neighborhood."

While acting somewhat mollified, Joe was still disturbed and said he had to insist that we sign over our deed to him. Matt said we would be willing to do that, knowing full well that an action performed under duress would not be legally binding, but our original deed was in a strongbox at our bank. Joe flew into a rage, "I demand that you sign something right here and now even if it is a handwritten declaration that the property belongs to Joseph W. Macintosh!" Matt said that was a fine idea but he'd have to have his hands free to write a document like that.

Joe balked at that suggestion. Apparently he suspected a trick and told Matt he'd have to think about it and while he was thinking he had a plan to entertain Matt. Then he turned his attention to me, approaching me and reaching out he began fondling my breasts through my night shirt. I said "Please wait, aren't we even going to discuss my options? If you are mean to me then I won't sign my portion of the deed and Matt and I are co-owners." "How is caressing you being mean to you?" Joe asked while saliva began to run down his chin.

That was when I screamed and kicked and Matt yelled "no" for all he was worth. The commotion caused our chairs to fall over tangling all three of us such that we fell on the floor. I, being thin and wiry, had managed to disengage my hands from the cuffs while Matt was being questioned. Now I broke free of the group and ran to the closest back exit. But when I arrived I realized with a shock how we had booby trapped the two closest doors in a futile attempt to keep Joe out. I could not get out without removing the blockade we had erected. I spun around, dodged the pursuing maniac, and headed for our bedroom.

I was quick despite just awaking from a drugged state; my terror of this man was a great motivator and he was probably never an athlete from the look of him nor was he worried about catching me as he was convinced that he held the upper hand. I got to the bedroom first and slammed the door shut behind me. I could hear him coming up the stairs almost laughing as he said "you won't escape me, I've almost got you!"

Once in the bedroom I dove into the walk-in closet also shutting that door behind me. I moved a few shoe boxes and unlatched the trapdoor. While this set of folding stairs had not been used much in years, I certainly knew how to let them down and in a moment I was in the cellar. I then sent the stairs back up thinking if Joe got as far as my closet and saw the trapdoor he might not know how to release the mechanism to allow the stairs to drop into place.

I had two thoughts: should I go up the stairs to the kitchen and try to rescue Matt before Joe would go back down there trying to catch me again or did I run out the bulkhead and reach help before Joe could find me? Then I saw a sight that would stop me cold.

Sybil, now a full grown cat, was with Scruffy. She must have dashed down here when Joe was pushing Scruffy down the stairs. Scruffy still seemed dazed but was very interested in what Sybil was doing for Sybil was madly scratching in the dirt of the cellar floor. At first I thought is this where Sybil finds a bathroom without using her box? But then I realized that Sybil was not trying to cover up a mess, she was trying to help something or someone to become unearthed!

I was pretty certain I was losing what was left of my mind for the next thing I saw was a claw-like skeletal hand emerging from the floor. But it wasn't that the cat had dug up a skeleton, it was that the cat had helped a hand to be freed while it was emerging from the ground. The "hand" was actually moving on its own and beginning to unearth more of its remains!

That was when I heard Joe coming down the trapdoor stairs behind me. I ran and hid inside the old chimney-hole where the original farmers used to store the ash for their soap. All I had to do was lean over and scurry into a dark corner and pray I wouldn't find a Goliath on my shoulder. Then I heard a terrorized scream. It was more than a scream but there are no words to describe the death knell rattling in the voice of a grown man as he was being pulled toward a hole in the ground by a skeleton!

I stepped out of the little room in the chimney base and stared in abject horror at the spot on the dirt floor where Sybil had been scratching. There was a battle going on between Joe and a boy sized skeleton. The skeleton was stronger with immeasurable power and snapped Joe in half and then began sucking on his limbs as though eating the legs on a boiled lobster. Joe screeched one more time and then was quiet.

It was then that I decided to run for Matt. As I began to mount the cellar stairs to the kitchen I glanced back at the death scene below and thought I saw another figure rising from the earth. I could not comprehend this and turned my attention back to the mission of rescuing Matt.

I had time to free him, with Sybil and Scruffy on my heels, and our little family made its way out the front of the house in just moments. Sergeant Parker was turning into our driveway at that very moment not anticipating being met by an hysterical couple and two dirt covered pets. Sergeant Parker was having trouble understanding what we were telling her but it sounded like Joe Mackintosh had just been murdered by a two hundred year old 12 year old boy who existed in our cellar.

29

SURVIVAL

Sergeant Parker tried to keep a straight face as she called this scene in to her command center at the State Police barracks. It was obvious, she said to them, that the Nelsons were distraught, especially Mrs. Nelson, but she did not quote us to Dispatch as it would have sounded as though she was the insane person here. She simply said there had been an invasion of some kind at the Nelsons' home on Cemetery Hill Road in East Apple and she would be investigating the scene. She also firmly called for backup assuming that Joe Macintosh might be injured somewhere on the premises and, she thought, that I might also require some medical services. The reason she had shown up was that she had been unable to get either of us to answer our morning check-in with her. Since the police patrol of our property had been instigated after the New Year's Eve fire she had checked in with us every morning. That was in addition to the patrol car coming by as scheduled.

Before back-up arrived Sergeant Parker said things seemed quiet enough for her to safely enter the home but just to follow protocol she asked us to sit in her car and she drew her weapon. She then entered the home loudly announcing herself and her rank. She went in the front door as Matt had advised her of the booby traps on the two side entries. She reported that once in the kitchen she saw her first signs of our story. Several chairs, ropes and even handcuffs were strewn about the room.

She also observed that the cellar door was ajar and noted that this was where I had specified that Joe Macintosh had perished. She went slowly down those shaky cellar stairs using her own flashlight as the switch did not seem to work. Again she announced herself and asked anyone down there to drop their weapon and come forward with their hands up. There was not a sound in response.

Then she said she cased every foot of that admittedly creepy old cellar. The only thing she would find out of place was that there was an unexpected set of trapdoor steps hanging down from the upstairs which was two stories above. She slowly ascended those steps and found herself in a clothing closet and then made her way through what was our master bedroom and then down a set of stairs eventually returning to the kitchen.

At this point she heard the backup response cars arrive and went out to brief them and us. She allowed her deputies to complete the examination of the house and she remained outside with us as we were having difficulty believing that there was no sign of Joe Macintosh or a killer skeleton.

But no matter how often we repeated our stories, both separately and together, we did not deviate from our original tale although we admitted to having been drugged. Also, I was the only one who actually claimed to have seen the skeleton and the demise of Joe. The deputies returned and reported no further findings.

In the next few weeks there were no additional sightings of Joe Macintosh. But we remained so unnerved that we decided to sell our dream home. On the day we were planning to call Adam to see what we should list the house for, given our work, a story came on the news. It featured a warning out of China from a few weeks back. It spoke of a horrible global pandemic which had already devastated Europe, including Italy, and was now killing people in the United States. It stated that everyone should remain in their homes for an indefinite period of time to help slow down the spread of this novel virus. It soon became clear to both of us that we could not plan to leave our home anytime soon.

Initially it did not seem possible that the entire world could be experiencing a horror of this magnitude, enough to make our own recent trauma seem almost reasonable, but in very short period of time a massive number of deaths were occurring with no clear end in sight. Slowly we began to accept that we really could not leave this home and then the questions arose as to how we could cope with staying here knowing what we knew about the bodies in the cellar.

Adam had said he could try and sell the place but that very few people were physically getting out and looking at homes. Further he advised that our home had just made the local papers for a "supernatural disappearance perhaps even linked to a death." He said "it would take several years for the publicity to die down enough for prospects to become interested in our home." His advice was that we simply "reframe our thoughts and enjoy the old place."

Matt seemed game but I was not and I could not even ask my folks to visit in order to gain their opinion as they had to remain isolated too.

30

UNRAVELING HISTORY

Early in the Pandemic lockdown I made a special request at our pharmacy. It was for a home pregnancy test kit. I thought it was probably the trauma of seeing the skeleton sucking on Joe's body that had caused my endocrine system to stop functioning normally but I had definitely missed my period. As Matt and I somehow still have a good love life, and I would love to have a baby, I figured I might as well find out. With mixed feelings of joy and fear I soon had the answer that I was, indeed, pregnant.

I wasn't afraid of having a baby but I was concerned about the impact of the virus risk for the baby and for me. I also had some trepidation regarding going to doctors' offices at this time but reasoned we will figure something out. Matt was overjoyed and so we both thought we had found the pot of gold lining this bleak time in history.

I was disappointed that we would have to announce the pregnancy to our parents via telephone. I had dreamed of my mother's excitement and wonderful hugs when the news came but the Covid 19 virus would not allow for close contact and especially across states and generations. So we shared the joy via Face Time. It was still fun but something was lost. Hopefully the virus would end in time for them to play with their new grandbaby right after he or she made an arrival.

Thus life had resumed some of its sparkle until I remembered the story of the widow placing a curse on male children born in this house. I repeated to Matt what Reverend Martin had told me. As the widow was taken away in custody she had yelled out that no male child born in the home built by Judge Rider could flourish beyond age 12. The widow hated the Judge for his harshness which she believed was responsible for the loss of her only son and so created this curse out of deep anger, desperation and frustration. The curse had so disturbed the Judge and his family that they sold the home as soon as they possibly could; before the curse had taken a child. Of course they had a son to protect so who could blame them. And the curse was certainly reinforced by Miss Emily's son who died a horrible death at age 12. Although technically it could be argued Will had not been born in that house, but he had been raised in it since he was two days old.

I decided one thing I could do on-line while locked-down was find out the number of male children who had been born in this home and at what age and in what manner had they met their ends. I began with Esther who inherited the house from her father, Reverend Wilbur and his second wife Emily who had owned the home at the time she had married the Reverend. Esther had brought three of her four daughters to live in the house, the oldest remaining at her parents' dairy farm. They had at first shared the house with Emily and their cousin Theodor, one of Levy's sons. Theodor was thirteen when he began living on the farm well before his Grandmother Emily's death, although he had worked there for several years prior to that.

It seems when Esther and her husband wanted to set their girls up for marriage they offered each of the three a choice parcel of the land left to them and they also had to offer an equal share to all of her sisters' children. Of the sisters' offspring only Theodor was interested in a share of the land. It seems hard to believe that anyone would turn down an inheritance but Ginny had remained in Boston which is where she raised her children. These children were apparently very sophisticated and traveled frequently to the continent. They demonstrated no interest in visiting East Apple, Connecticut let alone having a responsibility connected to the small town. And, except for Theodor, Levy's children had their own plans.

This meant that Esther's three, plus Theodor Mills, were the owners which I should study. Their tracts of land were fairly large. In fact Teddy subdivided his land after he inherited it and lived on one piece and apparently gave the other piece to Edwin Thompson who I recalled was the brother of Mrs. Bridgefield, the biological mother of Will. Edwin would have been a very old man when Theodor passed the land to him. How had they connected and what possessed Teddy to give him part of his inheritance? And, of course the bigger question was, who had raised children in the original farmhouse, our current home, and how had these children fared, especially the male offspring?

The records seemed to indicate that Esther and John Farmer remained in the farmhouse for many years and turned it over to their two youngest granddaughters who joined them as caretakers during their later years. Apparently these two were very loyal to each other and neither married. They remained in the farmhouse for approximately sixty years until the last one passed on about 1949.

Then a grand-niece named Rebecca lived in the house for many years surviving her husband and most of her kin. She was ninety-three at the time of her passing and had been there for fifty-five years. That was 2004 when she had died in a nursing home. Eventually the relatives' attorney put the farmhouse on the market. Several relatives had wanted to inherit it but only if it were an outright gift. Rebecca had failed to leave a will so all of her somewhat distant cousins were to inherit the place equally. Naturally that would not work out well. Therefore the lawyer, serving as executor, deemed that the property must be sold and the money divided among all interested parties. Thus it went on the market.

Of course since no one person was to gain a sizeable sum from this sale, none of them actually wanted to put any personal time or money into the upkeep of the property. When Rebecca was in the nursing home the house had already begun to deteriorate and as the years passed it got no better. There were small leaks in the roof and around some windows, the house was badly in need of painting; and the only modernization which had been done was back in the early 1950's. Rebecca had stopped cooking and mice had actually damaged the insides of her stove. Needless to say most of the house had lost its charm and grace with the best fireplace in the house boarded-up and actually hidden from view. The water in the cellar added to the negative value of the home if prospects were viewing it after a rainstorm. The outbuildings were even in poorer repair and the entire home appeared in despair. Little wonder, I thought, that no one wanted the place until we came along with our romantic view of the old.

As interesting as this story was it did nothing to provide an answer to the question of whether or not a son could be safely raised on this property. No children had actually been born here since the Riders time and the only other child to have been raised here was Will. Fear began to trickle its way down my now sweating back. "Dear

God, what will become of my baby" I whispered out loud, for all records pointed to no male children having lived in this home for over 200 years!

But I also wanted to continue my research, to see if I could understand more about Theodor and his gift to Mrs. Bridgefield's brother. I decided to pull up any liens or possible law suits that might be associated with the property in its entirety. And there it was, shortly after Emily Harrison Wilbur's disappearance Edwin Thompson had gotten a lawyer to sue her estate for a share of the property. He claimed that her "adopted" son, Will, was actually his nephew and therefore entitled to inherit the entire property. There was even a record signed by Emily early on where she had made this nephew of his her legal heir. Edwin Thompson said it was his duty to come forward on behalf of his family to claim a share.

Mind you his sister was long dead as was her son Will. The bankers involved had attempted to convince Thompson he had no viable claim but he persisted. It was at this point that Emily's step-grandson, Theodor, attempted to negotiate with Thompson who eventually settled for half the land that had been left to him. No one could speculate as to why Teddy had been so willing to give something to this mean spirited old codger but Teddy was known for having a kind heart and he had never fully recovered from the loss of his grandmother especially when her body was not recovered. There was talk that he simply didn't want any fuss so this gift settled the matter. Interesting and perhaps I understood his motivation far better than those who had never read Emily's diary.

I searched the deed on Thompson's piece of land wondering how long he had kept it and how he had disposed of it. Apparently he had been much younger than his sister and lived to be an old man. But shortly after he negotiated ownership of this land he too had passed on leaving the property to his middle-aged daughter who in turn gave it to her son, Albert Macintosh. From what I could determine the land was inherited by Albert's son and he and his wife had eventually built a home on it and moved into it with their two little boys. After a few years they also had a third son, this one born at home, was named Joseph because they considered him a miracle.

I looked away from the computer screen. I had found a male child born in a true sense on this land and I had recently witnessed his demise at the hands of Will's skeleton!

31

SINS OF THE MIRACULOUS

Tracing this history had been my idea to lessen anxiety with proof that other male children had been born here and gone forward to enjoy rich and wonderful lives. I had never truly entertained the possibility that the horror I had seen in our cellar was the demise of the next known male child of that home. How could we stay here? And if we must remain here how could we continue this pregnancy? I would not bear a child, good Catholic girl or not, who was destined to become either a monster or to be consumed by one. Surely Matt would understand this. I planned on having this difficult discussion as soon as possible so that abortion could remain a viable option. With that in mind I printed out all my notes for Matt to read that evening.

As I reviewed the various property owners for Matt with the conclusion that no one at or next to the house on estate property had borne a son, Matt appeared almost disinterested. But when I concluded with the information that Joseph Macintosh had been related to Edwin Thompson and had been born a few feet away from here he seemed to be listening more intently. Finally, my conclusion that the curse of our home had led to Joseph's craziness and had likely predicted that he must be the next victim of "the cellar", seemed to greatly disturb him. But not in the way I had wanted.

Matt was breathing unevenly and encouraging me to continue my thoughts. When I got to my pitch that we must find a way to leave or I would have to have an abortion he was on his feet shaking his head and a fist. He was angry and loud "You better get over this sleuthing of yours! I thought it was good to entertain you when I was doing research all the time. You never once complained because you had that diary of Emily's you were so obsessed with, always trying to read me passages that were frightening or supernatural or some other-world thing but this is different. Now you are talking about endangering the life of our unborn child; a tiny, innocent baby who just needs us to protect it be it boy or girl! You are really losing it Elena Maria you are off the deep-end and you need help. More help than I can give you!"

I became so frightened by his words; so totally unsupported and alone. All I could manage to say was, "Matt, if you are certain that this is all in my head I'd better just calm down and give my mind a chance to reconcile all that I've seen and read. Maybe I'm still suffering from posttraumatic shock and mixing things together. Also pregnancy hormones seem to bother some women. It will be okay Matt, I promise."

And he did seem to settle down. He asked if I'd mind if he had a glass of wine even though I could no longer drink and I was happy to serve him and prayed he would relax more. Tomorrow was soon enough for me to make a plan. Maybe my mother could advise me although I knew this would cause conflict within her too.

The next day we spoke on the phone and I must admit it put me in tears. The only thing different in this conversation was that my mother was immediately on my side; supportive, determined to help and proud of me for my courage. She also admitted that she had felt ill at ease since I announced my pregnancy; she was thrilled to become a nonna but she sensed a troubling circumstance might interfere with this plan. She hoped her sense was wrong but when I explained about the curse and Joseph she felt some external force telling her this was right, this was the problem.

She asked if I wanted her to come to me. I said, "Of course but how can you with this Pandemic going on?" Her reply was totally unselfish and so supportive. She said she was willing to remain in quarantine in my house for 14 days if I could provide her with food and leave one bathroom just for her use. She promised to be masked all the time and not to do anything foolish. She asked in return that Matt and I both get COVID tests and then we could be reasonably certain of safety. It made sense and became our plan. I didn't tell Matt why she was in such a hurry to join us but he seemed relieved to have help with "my mental health".

During her fourteen days of quarantine I sat on cushions outside my mother's door and we discussed many things. After a few hours I would get some exercise and cook a meal we could all enjoy and then do some work around the house. She read when I was busy and we both plotted how best to resolve the dilemma. We checked with my ObGyn regarding the earliest time to determine the gender of my baby. She and I agreed it would certainly put our minds at ease if I was carrying a girl. When it was okay to take the test I made an excuse to leave home and requested that the doctor's office leave word on only my cell phone with the answer. I confided that we needed to discuss a genetic disorder peculiar to males on my side of the family.

Then I went home to wait. Mother came out of quarantine the following day just as Dr. Kelly was calling with the results. "Well", she said, "I hope you can find a way to resolve your issue because you are carrying a boy. Let me know if I can set you up with a genetic counselor." I thanked her and promised to be back in touch. Then I sank to the floor and cried like a child with my head in my Mother's lap. We would have to do something horrible.

Matt knew nothing about the test and Mother and I faked our way through a pleasant meal, her first at the table with us. The next day she went down into the cellar with me. She had never questioned my experience down there but neither had she attempted to confront it in anyway. This time we sat together on the floor and then she leaned forward placing her hand where the mound of dirt, I recalled as the grave, was positioned.

She pulled her hand back very rapidly as though stung by something. I asked what had happened to which she replied "The energy under that soil is incredible and it is not of this world." When she suddenly crossed herself I did the same. We got up and waited until we were back upstairs before we spoke again. Then she said "Whatever you think is right to do I am with you and we must act soon!" I asked how soon and she would only repeat "soon".

I was truly frightened and so very sad but at least Mother was with me. The problem now would be where to get an abortion. I could call Planned Parenthood but I imagined there would be questions and I didn't think "fear of demonic spirits" probably qualified me for an abortion. Also, as each day passed my love for this little person seemed to grow. Wasn't there some chance that the curse had run out; that Joseph, actually born next door had genetic defects from his family that in no way related to the "curse"? Would I be killing a beautiful little angel who would have grown up to be loving and a bright light in this world? How could I murder this child?

I finally said all these things to my mother. She said she understood my hesitation, that of course such a decision would be traumatic, but I had to accept that the energy in the cellar was so evil that we could not let it take possession of my child. But she fully acknowledged that only I could make the final decision.

That night I had the worst nightmares of my life. Twice Matt shook me awake because I was crying or screaming and shaking the whole bed. All I could say to him, he said, was "My baby, my poor, poor baby." But I remembered more than I would say. The earth in the cellar bubbled open as though dirt could boil and from within that long ago grave appeared three human skeletal forms. The smallest one was apparently Will, the medium sized one was Emily and the one which still bore hanging flesh and some hair was Joseph. Joseph was angry but the other two sets of bones clearly held on to him, their powers were the stronger and he had no control around them. Before they disappeared back into the earth Emily spoke to me and in a horrible rasp she said "Hurry, you had better hurry!"

Did she mean hurry away? Run fast? Or did she mean get rid of that baby quickly before it is too late for all of you?

32

A MOTHER'S LOVE

Once Matt had left for the University, he was now working alone in his laboratory; I told mother all I had dreamt the night before. She was fascinated and said it was good that Emily cared more for us than she did for herself and Will. I asked how could she know that and exactly what did she mean? But she said, later darling, later, we will take care of this tonight.

I was a nervous wreck all day but managed to go through my usual motions functioning on automatic pilot. I wondered if this terror was what turned people into Zombies because I felt bloodless and half dead from worry. Fortunately Matt arrived home late, overworked and tired so that he went to bed early. My mother had been taking things into the cellar all day and once he was asleep upstairs she said we should go to work.

First we retrieved things hidden in the center chamber of the chimney: a shovel, a pick axe, a broom, a large tarp and a rake. Then we went to the assumed gravesite. My mother said that we would resolve once and for all what was in that earth. It was more work than I had expected since I believed it would not be firmly packed but loosened from much activity.

We took turns using the pick and then shoveling earth onto the tarp. After about forty minutes we hit a casket. This would be where Will's remains had been placed nearly 250 years ago. Near the casket was an intact set of bones wrapped in another tarp. We assumed these to be Emily, then with a bit of maneuvering we found a more recent corpse underneath hers. I wondered out loud how the most recent body got planted under Emily but my mother gave me a look that said, "You don't think they've been quiet do you?"

My mother's plan was to take them all outside and hide them in the barn. We would then fill the earth back in and rake over it to destroy the evidence that we had moved something. After Matt was gone in the morning we could decide what to do with the bones. In my mother's mind we removed the curse by removing the bones but she had forgotten the curse did not come from any activity associated with Will, it came from the widow enraged by the original owner of the home.

Still I had long wished to have these out of our cellar. But it was not so easy. As we leveraged Will's casket toward the tarp the cover deteriorated under our touch and hundreds of hideous spiders came rushing out. We behaved as I had read in Emily's diary, by pounding them in every direction until after much exertion and a little screaming, hoping not to wake Matt, they all lay dead or had vanished into the crevices of the cellar. Some had jumped at us, I had to claw one out of my hair and my desperation was so great that I ripped hair out with it. One may have stung my mother and they were making disgusting little squeaks similar to small pigs. Mother smashed the one that had bit her: she hit it even harder than the others until it too was not moving. We had run in circles throughout the cellar during this battle. Then, breathing heavily, we continued to place the bones on the tarp and collectively drag them up the bulkhead stairs and out into the yard, eventually into the barn.

We then went back into the cellar closing the outside door behind us, shoveling, raking and sweeping the earth until there were no signs of our efforts that night. My mother said I should now go to bed and she would be right up. She knew I would let Scruffy and Sybil out for a final time before we all went to sleep and then I would join Matt. She just wanted to take a last look around. A short-time later she ran into me in the upstairs hallway and whispered that the evil spirit was gone. She had sat by the dirt and felt no sense at all of an evil force. My baby was safe.

I slept well: no dreaming, no crying out but when I awoke to pee, at 3 A.M. as pregnant women do, I also had a strong urge to see my mother. I couldn't locate her in the pretty guest room we had given her across the hall from us. I reasoned she must have been having trouble sleeping after so much exertion. I went down to the ground level thinking I'd find her warming milk or sipping on chamomile tea. But the kitchen was quiet and when I touched the kettle it was cold. I said her name softly thinking she might be asleep on one of the parlor couches, but there were only pillows and Sybil who now decided to join in the search.

The last thing I wanted to do was to go down to the cellar alone with those horrid memories still so prominent in my mind. But now I had to find my mother. I got my giant flashlight out to help ensure good lighting and I also released Scruffy from his overnight crate and placed him on his leash. Then I opened the cellar door and made my way down the stairs. Whatever we had done to smooth over the grave site and whatever mother may have done for final repairs were done in vain. The dirt was strewn all over the cement part of the floor and there were muddy footprints leading up the bulkhead stairs. I had no choice but to follow them outside.

After a few seconds my eyes adjusted to the night light and I could see the glow of a fire on the backside of the barn. I carefully made my way around the barn keeping as close to it as possible to avoid revealing myself in the open. As I came around the far edge I saw the sight of a lunatic's fantasy for there were skeletons dancing around the fire and my mother was tied near-by. It appeared they might be preparing to roast her at the stake!

I cried out and the three skeletons all looked up. The medium sized bones, which I had presumed were Emily's, came forward. In a female voice but thick with anger it said "We are about to see that your mother can join us, after all she does know how to sense evil." And they all chortled. I stammered that I did not understand why this should be her fate. Then the medium bones said "Do not mistake me for one who cares, I am not your precious Emily, that grandson of hers could never bear to place her in the depth of the cellar. He left her in the ground at the church. I am the Widow who cursed this house and you know what I want. You are carrying a son for me."

"No," I cried, "You cannot take my son!"

"All right" answered the widow "Then I will take your mother!" And she gleefully galloped on her skeletal legs over to my mother where she dislodged her ropes and started pulling mother toward the flames.

I cried out "Please no I love her too dearly, you cannot take her!"

"Then the baby" said the hateful skeleton with the skull almost appearing to grin. And she released my mother's ropes and made leaps toward me. Just as she reached me my mother yelled "No, the child must live!" and she heroically threw herself into the flames. There was a burst of white light and she was gone.

I could not bear to watch or to remain with them for another moment. Sobbing and screaming I dragged Scruffy with me as we reentered the house and rushed upstairs to Matt. He grabbed me and held me until I could speak but once again he did not seem to believe me until he looked down and saw Scruffy drop a skeletal hand on his foot. He then rushed outside to survey the scene.

There was the unmistakable mark of fire on the ground but little else outside. He then reentered the house and called my mother's name several times. She was not to be found either in her bedroom or on the main floor. Finally, not wanting to believe what he was doing, Matt went into the cellar. He looked all around that large damp space for any clues. The only thing he found out of place was that there was a freshly made hump in the dirt which, to a superstitious eye could be viewed as a grave-like shape. And on top of the lump of soil was a silver baby's rattle. Mother had left us a gift.

EPILOGUE

Nothing had prepared me for the devastating loss of my mother. I saw her as my dearest friend and certainly my right hand during the pregnancy and the early months of raising our son. It never entered my mind that I could bring this baby into the world without her. But now we must, she had made that clear. Telling my father of mother's loss was also traumatic. He visualized her as having a sweet time with me as we knitted booties and shopped on-line for the infant. He was looking forward to their co-roles as grandparents and was even thinking of having the baby call him nonno to match with my mother's nonna. He just kept repeating "she cannot be gone" but, of course she was.

The State Police were another matter. They sent in all manner of detectives, scent dogs and CSI to determine my mother's whereabouts. The dogs did not sense any odor leading to the house and thus, due to COVID -19, they did not bring the dogs into the home. But I had seen mother disappear in a flash of white light out by the barn. The fire experts told me many times that no one ignites in that manner unless they were doused in an accelerant to which I refused agreement. That was just the way my mother burned: if it meant she was special than I could believe that but hoped to determine how this "special" would be labeled. Do angels go up in bright lights? And the expert forensic examination of our house only had evidence of my mother on the floors we had lived in, not even in the cellar.

Then there were the questions that only I worried over; why was the widow's skeleton in our cellar, had the Judge actually murdered her? Was that why he and his family left the house so quickly, because he had left a body in the basement? And what prevented dear, dependable Theodor from burying Emily in the cellar as she had requested? Did he run into someone or something down there the night Emily died, and did he carry guilt over not following her directions which led him to give half his inheritance away? And what of Emily's spirit, did she still seek to be laid to rest with Will? Could Matt and I do something for her?

As our baby moved inside me it strengthened my resolve to live and to even be happy. Matt was very tender toward me after the loss of mother and as he was overjoyed to be a dad. My father would join us as soon as a vaccine was available and that too would help our little family. I had much to live for and I knew as soon as the world was safer and the baby was thriving I would have to look into all the questions that still haunted me.

ADDENDUM TO THE BOOK

https://www.amazon.com/gp/product/1641844604/ref=ewc_pr_img_2?smid=ATVPDKIKX0DER&psc=1

If the reader will kindly go to this link, you will see stars and a rating area where customers are encouraged to rate this book. By rating it you will help others interested in horror and suspense. It also helps the author. Thank you, Cynthia H-B Adams